DISENGAGEMENT

Daniella Levy

Kasva Press

Make its bowls, ladles, jars and **pitchers** with which to offer libations; make them of pure gold.

תִּישְׁעוֹ
וִיתְרֹעֲקָ
וִיתְפֹלְכוֹ
וִיתוֹשִׁקוּ
וּלתיקֹנֹמוּ
דְסִי רֹשֹׁא
בְּהֹז זֹהֹב
הֹשׁעֹת רוֹהֹט
סֹתֹא

St. Paul / Alfei Menashe

An earlier version of the chapter titled "Neighbors" was published as a standalone piece under the title "Re-engagement" in the "New Neighbors" issue of *THEMA Literary Journal*, vol. 31, no. 1, Spring 2019.

Book design & layout: Yael Shahar

First edition published 2020
Kasva Press LLC
www.kasvapress.com
Alfei Menashe, Israel / St. Paul, Minnesota
info@kasvapress.com

Disengagement
ISBN
Paperback: 978-1-948403-13-9

9 8 7 6 5 4 3 2 1

DEDICATION

For Eitan,
because finding him
was finding home;

and in loving memory of my grandparents,
Alvin & Betty Shames,
who loved the land of Israel and her people all their lives.

CONTENTS

ISRAEL and the GAZA STRIP

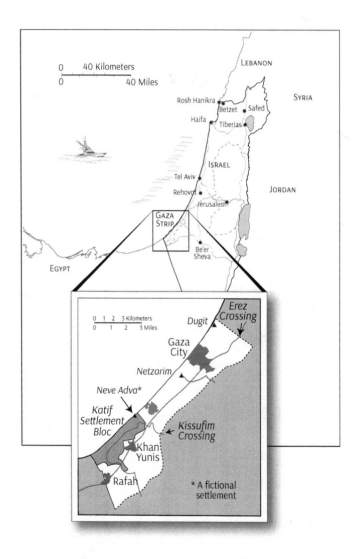

DISENGAGEMENT

Water and Sky

Maayan Tzurim

When a wine-red sun
Sinks into the sea
And scatters rays
In a thousand shades
Of orange and blue
The line that divides water and sky
Fades and is gone.
Where, then, do they meet?
Where does one
Become the other?

מַיִם וְשָׁמַיִם

מַעְיָן צוּרִים

כְּשֶׁשֶּׁמֶשׁ אַרְגָּמָן
שׁוֹקַעַת בַּיָּם
וּמְפַזֶּרֶת קַרְנֵי אוֹר
בְּאֶלֶף גְּוָנִים
שֶׁל כָּתֹם וּתְכֵלֶת
הַקַּו הַמַּפְרִיד בֵּין מַיִם לְשָׁמַיִם
הוֹלֵךְ לוֹ וְנֶעֱלָם.
הֵיכָן אָז נִפְגָּשִׁים הַשְּׁנַיִם?
הֵיכָן הָאֶחָד
הוֹפֵךְ לְמִשְׁנֵהוּ?

1

An Exasperated Clarification

July 27, 2004 | Ehud Hazan

This week I am forced to waste my precious corner of this publication on setting the record straight. Contrary to what many apparently deduced from the photograph of me that was printed in this paper yesterday, I did *not,* at any point, join Sunday's human chain to protest the evacuation of Gush Katif. Rest assured: every bone in my body supports the disengagement from Gaza. Please stop the emails.

I wasn't supposed to be anywhere near that event. Faithful readers of this column know that I prefer to steer clear of the settlements—geographically, ideologically, and in every other possible sense. My editor, however, wanted me to do some sleuthing regarding a mysterious figure connected to the protests, and no one else was available to do it. Svetlana Borokhov's name kept turning up in reports about the protest organization, but she never appeared in the media. Hoping to dig up some dirt on a mysterious shadow figure, he learned that she lived in Neve Adva—a Gaza settlement I'd never heard of—and wanted me to investigate.

Then why, you may be wondering, was I photographed carrying an orange-clad toddler off one of the buses transporting protesters to Yad Mordekhai Junction?

The answer is absurdly boring, but for the sake of dramatic tension, let's cut to a flashback: on the morning of the protest, around five kilometers past Kissufim Checkpoint, my car's engine did exactly what I should have done when Ginzberg assigned me this interview. It quit.

I must confess, I haven't spent much time beyond the Green Line. We Tel Avivim are often accused of living in a bubble, ignoring the chaos and violence of the Conflict until it arrives at our own doorstep; certainly in the last five years, it has arrived in all its gruesome glory. I'm sure you are all familiar with the morbid body count game we play. You're listening to the news, and you hear that there's been a terror attack. You tense up. Your first question is, "Where?" Somewhere far away from you. You relax. And if it's over the Green Line, you likely flip your hand in dismissal. Crazy shit has been going down out there since time immemorial. You don't have time to feel concern about this. You don't have the emotional energy to waste on those crazed religious fanatics choosing to make their homes in that hellhole. Then, one of these bone-chilling stories breaks through: a mother and her four little daughters, gunned down at point blank range. And you look at their photographs in the paper and try not to see the faces of your own wife and daughter and you console yourself: "That's what they get for living on stolen Palestinian land."

The calculation is different when you're stuck on the shoulder—if you could call it that—of the very highway that soaked up their blood.

As the car rolled to a stop, the mid-morning prayers blasted from the muezzins on either side of the road, as if to strengthen the point.

I was just starting to compose my own obituary when a station wagon pulled up in front of my car. The man who stepped out was swarthy and sported a long black beard flecked with gray. My grip on the steering wheel relaxed a bit when I noted that his plates were Israeli and that he was wearing a large knit kippa.

"Everything okay?" he asked when I rolled down the window.

"I think it's the engine," I replied.

"Pop the hood and let's take a look."

The man introduced himself as Shlomo. After determining that the car was a lost cause, I pulled out my phone to call a tow truck—but my cellphone had no reception.

"No one gets reception out here," Shlomo said with a shrug. "Come home with me. You can call whoever you need from there."

He hadn't even asked my name yet.

We had a more proper introduction once we were on our way. It turned out that he was none other than the rabbi of Neve Adva, Shlomo Toledano. When I told him who I was, the corners of his mouth tensed a little.

"Ehud Hazan," he repeated. "You're that left-wing columnist who writes for all the papers about how great it is that the government's planning to throw me out of my home."

"Guilty as charged," I said. "I hope you're not planning to throw me out of your car now."

He didn't, but he didn't say he wouldn't, either.

I broke the awkward silence that followed by asking him about Svetlana Borokhov.

"Svetka? You want to interview Svetka?" He glanced at me. "Do you speak Russian?"

"No."

He raised his eyebrows. "Well, good luck."

"Does she not speak Hebrew?"

"Not very well. And from what I know of her, she hates reporters."

This did not bode well for Ginzberg's big scoop.

Neve Adva is a tiny seaside settlement not far from Neve Dekalim. Like all Jewish settlements in Gaza, Sharon's disengagement plan slates it for evacuation. It comprises some twenty-odd homes lined up in two neat rows facing the shore; most made of stone, with multiple stories, rooftop balconies, and generous patios facing the sea. Some are caravans — the tin mobile homes with flat fiberglass roofs — and some are a hybrid, permanent stone structures built around or alongside a caravan. The area around the homes is mostly sand, and mostly littered with plastic toys. There was a small but colorful garden next to Rabbi Shlomo's driveway, with bright geraniums, succulents, and herbs. Rabbi Shlomo batted away a tendril-like branch of purple bougainvillea as he led me to his door.

The living room was spacious and tastefully decorated; the walls were painted in shades of cream and hazelnut brown, and a plump leather couch framed a dark wood coffee table that rested on a deep red oriental rug.

I couldn't help thinking: what a shame, to knock this thing down, when starving journalists in Tel Aviv are crammed into sardine cans along Tchernikovsky Street. What I wouldn't give for a huge house on an idyllic beach like Rabbi Shlomo's.

Then I remembered that the nearest decent supermarket was about twenty minutes and five hostile Arab villages away.

Rabbi Shlomo poured me a glass of ice water while I argued

with the tow company over the landline. It took them an hour to find a tow truck driver willing to cross the Green Line, and the one who finally agreed wouldn't make it until later that afternoon.

Rabbi Shlomo offered me a beer after I slammed down the phone for the fifth time, and invited me to stretch out on his couch. He pulled a curtain back over the bay window, revealing a spectacular view of the beach before cracking open a bottle and handing it to me.

"Where do you live?" he asked.

"I'll give you three guesses." I closed my eyes and rested the sweating glass against my forehead.

"So, Tel Aviv."

"Bingo."

"Well, you have a few options." He popped open his own bottle and took a sip, settling into the armchair across from the couch. "You can take the bus to Be'er Sheva, but frankly no one knows when it comes, because around here, if you don't drive, you hitchhike."

"Hitchhike?"

"That's your second option." He nodded, apparently not detecting the note of trepidation in my voice. "In other circumstances, it would be the one I'd recommend."

"And today's circumstances?"

"You know about the human chain tonight, I assume?"

"You assume correctly."

"There's a bus taking us all to our section near Yad Mordekhai on Route 4 this evening. You could come and try to get a ride with someone heading north." His eyes twinkled a bit as he took another sip of beer. "Unless, of course, you'd like to stay and protest with us."

I snorted, sending some beer up my nose.

Rabbi Shlomo pointed me to the Borokhov household and I made a few attempts to speak to Svetlana, but when her husband threatened to call the police, I figured I'd head back to Rabbi Shlomo's air conditioning. I ended up spending most of the day in the rabbi's house. At some point a bleary-eyed teenager emerged from one of the bedrooms, but he wasn't much of a conversationalist. As the air began to cool towards late afternoon, Rabbi Shlomo took me on a little tour to get a better look at Neve Adva. At the center of the settlement was a grassy area surrounding the synagogue: a small, flat-roofed building with peeling stucco walls, exposed rebar jutting out of the top, and—oddly—some half-hearted colored tiling around a varnished wooden door. It looked as though someone had tried to fix the place up and given up in the middle. A few small children were climbing on a worn wooden playground structure nearby. Mothers watched wearily from benches lining the park.

Next, Rabbi Shlomo took me to see the four greenhouses at the far end of the settlement and to introduce me to the farmers who ran them. Moshe Skolnik, like Rabbi Shlomo, was among the founders of Neve Adva and had been living there since 1993; his father Itzik, a Holocaust survivor, owned a farm in Katif until several years ago when his failing health forced him to sell it and move in with his son. They showed me verdant rows of cherry tomatoes, peppers, and lettuce.

As we headed back toward the synagogue, I noticed the minarets of the neighboring Palestinian village poking above the hill beyond the barbed-wire fence.

When we approached, the residents of Neve Adva were assembling in the park by the synagogue to wait for the bus. They were all decked out in that ghastly shade of neon orange worn by those who support Gush Katif. Rabbi Shlomo's wife Shulamit was there—and so, I noticed, was Svetlana Borokhov: the frail-looking woman with strawberry-blond hair and very pale skin I had glimpsed through the window before her husband chased me away. I began to approach her, but Shulamit planted herself in front of me.

"May I ask you a favor?" she asked.

She pointed to a house on the far end of the street.

"The woman who lives there was widowed last year," Shulamit said. "She has four kids and I bet she's struggling to get them out of the house. Would you mind...?"

I gawked at her. My own sister wouldn't let me babysit my nieces even if I had been remotely interested; but after Shulamit's husband had babysat *me* all day, I wasn't in much of a position to refuse, was I?

The widow's name was Talia and she was close to tears when I knocked on her door. When I mumbled that Shulamit had sent me to help her, she asked no questions; she merely shoved a screaming toddler into my arms and turned back into the house to deal with whatever other crisis was unfolding in her kitchen.

The toddler stopped crying, probably out of pure shock, and stared at me. For lack of better ideas of what to do with her, I stared back. She was wearing an orange shirt and a diaper. Nothing else.

"So how do you get away with not wearing pants?" I asked her. She did not seem inclined to explain.

Five minutes later, Talia returned to the doorstep to find us still sizing each other up. She glanced from the kid to me and said, "She likes you."

"That's because she doesn't read *Haaretz*," I said.

Ignoring my comment, Talia shut her door, not bothering to lock it, and herded us all toward the bus.

———————————————

And that, my friends, is how I ended up climbing off that bus with the toddler—who refused to let go of me the entire ride.

One of my colleagues was driving along the road to report on the protest, and he spotted me on the shoulder of the highway still trying to pry the little girl off my leg. He rescued me from her clutches and took me home to my sardine can—sniggering the whole way.

Didn't I warn you it was boring?

You may now all relax and quit with the hate mail. I might have discovered some slight potential for a future career in babysitting once Ginzberg finally fires me, but I promise you, I am just as left-wing and ornery as ever. You all need a vacation.

TWO OUT OF THREE

Summer 1993

The first time Rabbi Shlomo Toledano set eyes on the beach that would later be known as Neve Adva was much like the moment he first laid eyes on the woman who would later become his wife: an instant, inexplicable recognition wrapped in a sense of destiny, washing over him like his grandmother's perfume.

As he pulled up along the dirt road, the sun was beginning to kiss the edge of the horizon, scattering orange glitter over the blue Mediterranean. He stopped the car and cut the engine, squinting into the sun as he shoved open the door of his beat-up Hyundai station wagon and stepped onto the sand with his good leg. Stumbling away from the car — slipping a little as the sand shifted beneath his feet — he slammed the door shut and drew a deep draft of briny air.

Yes...he had felt this before, this profound stirring of familiarity that seemed just beyond the reaches of his memory. He first saw Shulamit at a classmate's wedding; she was just standing there among all the other young women, looking intently ahead at the wedding ceremony in progress. She never met his eye, never spoke to him; their paths did not cross during the rest of the evening. But he could not get her face out of his mind. He asked around at the yeshiva to try and found out her name, and when he found out that it was Shulamit, the image in his mind was soon accompanied by a soundtrack echoing in his head: Shulamit and Shlomo. Shlomo and Shulamit. Like characters from a fairy tale.

When he approached his spiritual advisor from the Har Etzion Yeshiva, Rabbi Yonatan had quoted the Talmud: "There are three graces: the grace of a wife to her husband, the grace of a hometown to its inhabitants, and the grace of an acquired item to its purchaser."

"What does 'grace' mean in that context?" Shlomo had asked.

Rabbi Yonatan smiled: "It's when you look at something and know instantly that it is destined to be yours — and you'll never be able to explain why."

———— ∾∾ ————

Indeed, when the kids were in bed that evening and he sat on the living room sofa with his wife and tried to explain why they should move into a trailer on a godforsaken beach in the middle of nowhere, the words would not come. There was a pause as long as the Exile when he finished telling her his conclusion. She just sat there staring at him, her coffee untouched on the glass coffee table, until she finally cleared her throat.

"But electricity, Shlomo," she said.

He nodded, but said nothing.

"But running water, Shlomo."

"They'll hook it up before we move down. They're laying the lines now."

"But the schools, Shlomo. Yossi is only five; you want to bus him to kindergarten in Neve Dekalim on those dangerous roads? It's bad enough with the girls hitchhiking to Dolev when they miss their bus."

Shlomo was silent.

"But your leg, Shlomo," Shulamit went on, glancing down at the exposed plastic foot resting on the faded maroon rug. "How will you manage the rough terrain? What about accessibility?"

"Everything there is flat. It'll be easier than climbing the stairs to this apartment on Shabbat."

Shulamit shook her head, looking down at her coffee, and then looked up again.

"But my job, Shlomo."

"You can apply at Soroka. Everybody needs more nurses."

"And what about the neighbors? We don't even know who they'll be. Frankly, I'm surprised you're not more concerned about the fact that it won't be a strictly religious settlement."

"Ariel is mixed."

"Ariel is different. Ariel is huge. We have everything we need here, and easy access to your parents in Lod. Tiny settlements like that are very close-knit, because they have to support each other. Imagine what Shabbat will be like if the kids don't have any —"

"But the *quiet*, Shulamit," Shlomo blurted, and Shulamit fell silent. "The *quiet*, the open air, the open sky..." he trailed off with a helpless gesture.

Shulamit sighed, reaching up to unwrap the scarf from around her hair.

"There's at least one other religious family with kids signed up," Shlomo went on. "The girls are older now, they're more independent. If they're bored on Shabbat they can go stay with friends. And the settlement will grow. And we'll adapt. We have to move there, Shulamit. We have to."

She looked up into his eyes and scrutinized him, unpinning her hair and letting the soft, graying brown locks fall about her shoulders.

"There will be no talking you out of this, will there," she said. It was not a question. She sighed and rubbed her forehead. "God help us."

Rabbi Shlomo timed his family's first glimpse of their new home so they would see it as he had seen it: as the sun was beginning to set. They piled out of the car onto the freshly laid asphalt in front of the caravan, and the girls immediately kicked off their sandals and ran around the caravan toward the waterfront, giggling and whooping.

"Come on, Yossi!" Orit, the eight-year-old, called to the five-year-old boy, who hung back, clinging to Shulamit's skirt. "Come see the water!"

"Oh, Ima, can we sleep out here tonight, under the stars?" fourteen-year-old Vered swooned, spreading her arms wide and twirling so her full, ankle-length skirt flared around her.

Shulamit laughed. "You can sleep wherever you want," she said, "but I'd rather not wake up with the whole beach in my pajamas."

Twelve-year-old Reut finally coaxed Yossi away from Shulamit and led him by the hand toward the shore. Shlomo watched the silhouette of his children standing holding hands where the sea met the land, and his heart filled with that feeling again. *Grace.* He peeked at Shulamit, standing there with her gaze ahead, just like she was doing at the wedding where he first saw her. He glanced around at the other caravans to see if anyone was watching before slipping his hand mischievously into hers. She giggled and blushed a little. They never touched in public.

He leaned toward her, breathing in the scent of her shampoo.

"Welcome home, my love," he whispered into her ear.

The next morning, Rabbi Shlomo wandered over to the row of greenhouses that had been erected near the fence. He found a wiry man with a little kippa hanging haphazardly from a single alligator clip, unloading small plastic planters from the bed of a pickup truck.

"Shalom, neighbor," Rabbi Shlomo called. The man turned at the entrance to the greenhouse, squinting in Rabbi Shlomo's direction.

"Aleichem shalom," he returned, shifting the planters to one arm and extending a hand. Rabbi Shlomo shook it, and then withdrew his own hand and kissed it.

"Shlomo Toledano."

"Ahh, you're the rabbi who moved in two caravans down," said the man, leaning back to size him up. "I'm Moshe Skolnik."

"Here." Shlomo reached for one of the stacks of planters, took it from Moshe, and walked him into the greenhouse. He coughed at the sudden blast of moist, hot air. "What are you planting?"

"Oh, these? Geraniums," said Moshe. He pointed at a row of sticks jutting out from the ground. "Cherry tomatoes here, bell peppers there. My wife wanted some flowers too. Geraniums grow beautifully in Gaza."

"Is this your first farm?" Shlomo asked, bending to lower the planters to the ground.

"Sort of." Moshe squatted and began arranging the planters in rows. "My father owns some land up near Katif, so I grew up in the business."

"Sorry I'm not . . . helping more," Shlomo said. "I would, but . . . my leg." Moshe glanced up at him, and he lifted the hem of his right pant leg to reveal the plastic.

Moshe shook his head in sympathy. "What happened to it?"

"Hand grenade. The other half is in Lebanon somewhere. Is it just you here, or do you have help?"

"At the moment I have my wife and Aharon Cohen, the guy who lives in the caravan between yours and mine," Moshe replied, jumping up to drag a sack of soil over to the planters. "But Bruria's actually in the village now interviewing some workers to hire."

"Arabs?" Rabbi Shlomo blinked.

Moshe laughed, shaking soil from the bag into the planters. "Of course."

Rabbi Shlomo stroked his beard absently.

"Is that...common?" he ventured.

"Not as common as it used to be. My parents moved to Gaza in the early days after the war. They got along well with the 'cousins' back then. My father went to the dentist in Gaza City."

Rabbi Shlomo tried to imagine lying in a dentist's chair and opening his mouth to let a Palestinian with a drill at his teeth. He shuddered.

"It was only after the intifada started — '87, '88 — that things started to get bad. We'll need an armed guard to watch them." Moshe started packing down the dirt. "Hopefully, when this place grows a bit, we'll be able to start hiring more locals."

The honeymoon phase faded quickly as the difficulties of isolation set in. Shulamit had to wake up before dawn to make her bus to Be'er Sheva, and it took a while for the regional council to arrange a bulletproof bus to bring the little ones to their schools in Neve Dekalim. Rabbi Shlomo spent his morning and early afternoon chauffeuring them back and forth — stopping at the synagogue to pray along the way, since there weren't enough men in their new settlement to make up a proper quorum. The older girls stayed in the dorms of their high school in Dolev, coming home only for the weekends. Shulamit often arrived home after nightfall from her shift at Soroka, so it fell to Rabbi Shlomo to take care of household chores, do the shopping, and entertain Orit and Yossi in the afternoons. Once he came home from the morning drop-off and services, though, he was free to spend the morning walking along the beach and getting to know the neighbors.

Their first Sabbath in Neve Adva, Rabbi Shlomo invited the man in the caravan next to theirs for the Friday night meal. With the girls home, even the addition of a single guest made the living room feel crowded. Aharon Cohen was a young man fresh out of *hesder* who turned out to have studied in the same yeshiva as Rabbi Shlomo, so they exchanged stories about their teachers over Shulamit's rich chicken soup. When their reminiscing quieted, Shulamit came out with that most beloved question of Jewish housewives:

"So Aharon, are you dating anybody?"

Aharon blushed a deep red, and that's when they learned that one of the reasons he'd moved to Neve Adva was that he had just gotten engaged and wanted to seize the housing opportunity.

"Kululu!" Shulamit ululated, and the older girls burst into a rendition of *Od Yishama* as Rabbi Shlomo clapped along and Aharon turned even redder.

"I'm sure you'll want one of your rabbanim from yeshiva to officiate at the wedding," Rabbi Shlomo said, "but just so you know, I'm certified as well, and I'd be happy to do it for you here."

"We were thinking about doing it here, actually," Aharon said. "I will have to ask—"

At that moment, the lights blinked off.

"Ima, what happened to the lights?" came Yossi's startled voice.

"It's nothing, just a power shortage," Shulamit reassured him. "I'm sure the power will come back on soon. In the meantime, good thing we have Sabbath candles!" The candles flickering on the countertop did cast enough of a glow through the room for them to continue their meal in peace, but the power did not come back on, and without the fans blowing, the heat became stifling.

Rabbi Shlomo tossed and turned in bed, the stump of his missing leg swollen and throbbing and itchy from the sweat. Finally, he pulled himself out of bed and leaned on the walls and furniture for balance as he made his way outside, not bothering to strap on his prosthesis. The sea breeze offered immediate relief, and he stretched out on his back in the sand. Above him stretched a magnificent sky studded with stars — brighter and more numerous than he'd ever seen them. And though he was exhausted and uncomfortable and his phantom limb was tingling, he smiled at the Heavens.

"All right, Hashem," he whispered. "That covers two out of three graces. I'm willing to compromise on the third, as long as I get to keep these two."

The stars twinkled in response.

MIRROR IMAGE

Spring 1995

*C*hange your place — *change your luck.*

That's the Hebrew saying that popped into Svetlana Borokhov's mind when she saw those two lines on the pregnancy test and suppressed a sob borne of elation, relief, and anxiety all mixed together.

"Mickey," she called, trying to restrain the emotion in her voice. He was in the bedroom across the caravan, and thin as the walls were, he had always slept like a bear. She lifted the test from the sink as though it might crumble in her hands at any moment, and raised her eyes to the mirror. She hardly recognized the face staring back at her — bloated and pockmarked from the hormone treatments and the subsequent acne. Before she had started fertility treatments, whenever she looked in the mirror, she saw the face of her twin, Olga. Since they were little girls, they mirrored each other's lives, too; like storybook twins with their identical strawberry-blonde pigtails and piercing green eyes, they played switcheroo pranks on their teachers back in Moscow, followed their Jewish mother to Israel the minute President Gorbachev lifted the ban on emigration, married a pair of cousins and moved to Dugit — and then, just a few weeks ago, to Neve Adva. Now, for the first time in their lives, they were easy to tell apart: Olga was the one with the belly swollen with her second child, and Svetka was the one swollen everywhere else.

Svetka tiptoed to the bedroom and peered in at the mass that was Mickey, his chest rising and falling gently. She lingered for a moment, and then decided not to wake him. Instead, she stepped out of the caravan and walked to the next one over, knocking gently on the door. Olga, who was always up at this hour, opened it, and Svetka held up the stick, laughing a little as she blinked away tears.

"Oh, Svetka!" Olga threw her arms around her sister, and when she pulled back, she examined the stick with wide eyes. "Oh, Svetka," she repeated, and then wrapped her twin in a hug again.

———

The Neve Adva they had just moved to had changed a lot in the two years since its founding. Several more rows of caravans had been added, and permanent buildings were coming up: a modest synagogue in the center, with several homes under construction on the beachfront — including those that Mickey and Baruch were building for their respective families. When Mickey suggested that perhaps they wouldn't need quite as much room as Baruch and Olga, Svetka refused to speak to him for a week. There would be three bedrooms, she insisted, with the option of adding more on the top floor if necessary. They had the money. Mickey bit his tongue and did as she said.

In the meantime, Svetka started a small daycare out of one of the vacant caravans. She couldn't believe people were willing to pay her to snuggle their babies all day. In the weeks after she learned she was pregnant, she hugged them close, breathed in their baby-detergent scent, and closed her eyes, dreaming of the baby she couldn't hold yet.

In the years since Kinneret's birth and especially since Svetka had begun fertility treatments, conversations with Olga didn't flow as easily as they used to. It happened so slowly that she didn't really notice the tension in their voices or the long pauses in conversation until they stopped. Now there were ultrasounds and blood tests to chat about, and shopping trips in Be'er Sheva to buy baby things together. One of the things that had pained Svetka about failing to get pregnant had been the understanding that she wouldn't be able to give Kinneret a cousin her own age. But she was only six months behind Olga now, and as she watched Kinneret running along the beach, throwing stones into the water, Svetka pictured her unborn nephew and child trailing after Kinneret together, collecting seashells.

She held on to that image when she saw the wrinkle in the doctor's forehead at the routine ultrasound scan at thirteen weeks. Her Hebrew wasn't quite as good as Mickey's, and she couldn't concentrate hard enough to fully understand what the doctor said as she climbed off the table and he typed into the computer. She sat on the bus from Ashkelon to Gush Katif staring at the words on the printed report, trying to discern what they meant. There were notes printed in English beneath the Hebrew, but they didn't help. When she arrived in Neve Adva she took the report out to the dock Mickey and Baruch were building for their fishing boats. Mickey was up to his waist in the surf, bare-chested, hammering nails into one of the wooden posts, and he froze when he saw Svetka approaching. She didn't say a word, but he immediately waded toward the shore, tossed the hammer into his toolbox and approached her. She handed the paper to him.

"I don't understand what it says," she said, her voice trembling. "Something is wrong, but I don't know what."

Mickey studied the paper, sighed deeply, and shook his head. "I don't know either. Isn't the rabbi's wife a nurse? Let's take it to her this evening."

Shulamit Toledano invited the couple to sit on the plastic chairs outside her caravan as she squinted at the report. Svetka's heart sank as she saw that same wrinkle appear in her brow below the large maroon headscarf concealing Shulamit's hair.

"Your cervix," she said. "It's shorter than it should be."

"What does that mean?" Mickey asked.

"It means you're at risk of premature labor. The baby seems to be fine, *baruch* Hashem." She handed the page back to Svetka. "He says you should be on bed rest."

Mickey and Svetka exchanged glances. Svetka could not speak. She stared at the ground, willing herself not to cry in front of her neighbor.

"You need to see him again in two weeks. Do you want me to help you find someone to cover for you at the daycare in the meantime?"

"Olga took over today..." Mickey said.

"Olga is due any day now," Svetka whispered in Russian. "We can't rely on her."

"We'll find someone." Shulamit reached across the table to take Svetka by the arm, and at her comforting touch, Svetka could hold the tears back no longer.

"I can't lose this baby," she sobbed. "I can't. She might be the only chance I have."

She was speaking Russian, and she knew Shulamit couldn't understand the words, but Shulamit scooted her chair around the table and put her arm around Svetka.

"I know this is scary," she said in Hebrew, her voice soothing, "but I know many women who carried to term with a diagnosis like this. Don't despair now. Come on, let's get you home and into bed. I'll find someone to take over the daycare, and I'll ask Batya about setting up meals for you. All you need to do is keep that baby in there. Okay?"

Svetka just nodded, fiercely rubbing the tears away.

She never made it to her appointment two weeks later.

Three days after the ultrasound, she woke from a nap with a sharp pain in her middle. She gasped, grabbing at her abdomen, and noticed that her legs felt wet and warm. She looked down and suppressed a scream. Her sheets were covered in blood.

She jumped out of bed, her mind racing. *What do I do? What do I do?*

"Mickey," she called out, but then remembered that he had taken the truck to Be'er Sheva for fishing supplies. "Olga!"

She stumbled across the caravan, pulling open the door. Olga was outside with Kinneret, and she screamed at the sight of her sister trailing blood.

"The baby," Svetka gasped, and clutched her abdomen as another sharp pain overtook her.

In the fog of pain, she heard her sister's voice, strong and clear: "Go get in my car. I'll get towels."

Driving to Kissufim Checkpoint had become scarier since the Oslo Accords the previous year, and under normal circumstances, Svetka was gripped by anxiety whenever they exited the gate of

23

Neve Adva. But now she noticed nothing; not the new red signs warning Israelis not to enter the Palestinian villages; not the whining of her niece from the back seat; not her sister, lips pressed into a thin line, knuckles white as she gripped the steering wheel. All she knew was the pain, sharp, throbbing, seizing her belly in waves; the slippery wetness between her legs; and the tightness in her chest whenever the pain subsided and her mind was clear enough to think.

I can't. I can't. I can't lose this baby.

By the time they reached Soroka Hospital, Svetka was white as plaster and her vision was swimming. She felt Olga's rough grip on her arm, pulling her out of the passenger's seat with Kinneret balanced on one hip. She allowed herself to be led into the emergency room, and soon there were voices, other hands touching her, pulling her, leading her away. Svetka caught a glimpse of Olga's huge belly before the sisters separated, not exchanging a word.

Svetka's eyes fluttered open, startled a little by the electronic beeps representing her own heartbeat. Her head felt heavy and a wave of nausea overtook her, making her wince. A hand that had been holding hers tightened its grip, and she flicked her eyes over to where Mickey sat. He gave her a tired smile. His eyes were bloodshot, and the wrinkles around them seemed deeper than she remembered.

He swallowed.

"How are you feeling?" he asked, and there was a tension in his voice.

She searched him suspiciously.

"What aren't you telling me?" she rasped. Her throat felt raw.

He lowered his eyes. "Olga went into labor while they were prepping you for the evacuation procedure," he said, his voice barely audible. "It's a boy. They're both fine."

Svetka closed her eyes, and a stream of tears flowed on either side of her face.

"It's not fair," she choked. "It's just not fair."

LABOR

Summer 1997

Aharon Cohen lay awake, gazing at the relaxed, angelic faces opposite him on the bed. His tiny daughter lay on her back with her arms splayed, forcing her mother into a narrow sliver of the bed by the wall, with one arm curved over the baby's head. A bright yellow patch of sunlight streaming in from the window was creeping toward Emuna's hair — deep red fluff she'd inherited from him. Talia's dark strands were blowing gently across their faces in the breeze from the fan at the foot of the bed.

Aharon reached behind him to adjust the blinds. It had been a long night, and he didn't want the sun to wake them before Emuna's hunger did.

He sat up as gently as he could, wincing and rubbing his upper arms to ease the soreness in his muscles. Then he stood up, grabbed his *tzitzit* and kippah from his nightstand, and tried to tiptoe into the main room of the caravan without making the floor creak too badly.

As he filled the kettle and switched it on, he studied the canvas Talia had left on the table; a blur of blues and greens filled the upper portion, while the rest was left blank. He poured the boiled water into a thermos with two spoonfuls of instant coffee, wondering whether she had taken the painting out in hopes of getting back to it. It had been two months since she'd painted anything — she had been fully occupied with a different creative endeavor. He guessed her hands must be missing the paintbrushes now, though.

He glanced at the painting that hung on the wall: a simple watercolor of an alley in Safed with a stained-glass door. Not her greatest masterpiece, but special to them nonetheless: it was the piece she'd been painting when he first spotted her, sitting in that alley with her hair tied back, hunched over the canvas, eyebrows knit in concentration. He'd stopped to watch, and when she sat up straight and protested that he was making her nervous, he asked her where she'd learned to paint like that. She shrugged, and he told her that his sister studied at a fine-arts academy for religious women in Jerusalem. He offered to write down its name for her, and as an afterthought he scribbled his own name and number beneath it. She took the note from him without comment and went back to work. After a few moments of waiting for a reaction, Aharon gave up and went on his way.

Talia didn't work up the nerve to contact him until four years later when she'd almost graduated that academy. She had finally confessed to Rabbanit Oriya, her favorite teacher at the seminary she'd attended in Safed, that she'd kept Aharon's number all those years but never dared to call him; and the rabbanit told her bluntly to stop being a coward. Aharon had to resist the urge to hug the woman when she showed up at their wedding.

He found himself smiling idly as he stirred in the sugar and screwed the cap onto the thermos. He stole another glance at his wife and daughter before leaving the caravan. They still slept, their chests rising and falling in a synchronous rhythm.

When Aharon arrived at the greenhouse after the morning prayers, Yusuf and Mohammad were waiting by the door, their T-shirts already stripped off and their bare browned chests already glistening with sweat. They were casting sidelong glances at the IDF soldier standing several paces away with an M-16 slung over his shoulder. But Yusuf caught sight of Aharon and smiled.

"*Boker tov, habibi*," said Yusuf. "How are you?"

"*Sabah an-noor*," Aharon returned. "Thank God. And you?"

"Aharon! *Ma nishma?*" the young soldier called out.

Aharon turned toward him. "Pini! Nice to see you back here!" He approached Pini, returning his broad smile, and clapped him on the shoulder.

"How's your wife? Did she have that baby yet?"

"Yes, *baruch* Hashem, she gave birth two months ago."

"Oh, mazal tov! Boy or girl?"

"Girl." Aharon smiled and drew a photograph of Emuna from his pocket.

To Pini's credit — he was, after all, a nineteen-year-old who probably could not have cared less about babies — he examined the photo with convincing interest. "So sweet," he said, handing the picture back. "Listen, do you have a cigarette by any chance?"

Aharon drew out a box and handed him one, then placed another in his own mouth and patted his pockets, looking for a lighter.

"Need a light?" came a gruff voice from behind them. It was Mohammad, holding up a small plastic lighter.

Pini and Aharon both eyed him warily. Aharon had been working side by side with Yusuf for years and was used to him; they were even quite friendly, bantering in Yusuf's broken Hebrew, drinking coffee together with the other Arab worker, Khalid. But Khalid got married and moved to Nablus, and Mohammad had replaced him several weeks ago, and ... after all, they *were* Arabs.

"Thank you," Aharon said, slowly lifting his cigarette to the lighter. Mohammad struck it alight, shielding the flame from the wind with his other hand. Pini did not follow Aharon's lead.

Aharon paused, staring at the lit end of his cigarette, then tentatively lifted the rest of the pack. "Do you want one too?" he offered. It seemed only polite.

Mohammad nodded and drew one from the box, sticking it in his mouth and lighting it. Pini finally gave in and held out his cigarette as well; Mohammad lit it without a word.

Mohammad sucked on the cigarette, giving Aharon a piercing look. "Your wife had a baby girl?" he said finally in his heavily accented Hebrew.

Aharon hesitated a moment; should he really share personal information with an Arab? Well, he reasoned, what harm would there be in answering honestly? It wasn't like he was inviting the man to come visit his home. He nodded in the affirmative.

Mohammad drew a picture out of his own pocket and handed it to Aharon. A woman in a cream-colored hijab smiled shyly from the photograph, cradling a newborn baby. "Mine too," Mohammad said. "A great blessing, a little girl." He took the picture back and examined it. "Sons are good. She gave me three. But daughters are the sweetest things." He looked up at Aharon, a soft look in his eyes. "She's a sweet one, my Amal."

Aharon found himself taking his own photograph out of his pocket and handing it to Mohammad. "My Emuna," he said.

"Good morning," came Moshe's voice from behind them, and Mohammad returned Aharon's photo as Moshe unlocked the greenhouse door.

At around 10 o'clock, the greenhouse workers ducked outside again for a coffee break. Aharon wiped at the sweat dripping from his forehead and dropped the large garden shears he'd been using on the ground. Pini, who had been standing guard outside the greenhouse and looking profoundly bored all morning, perked up.

"How's it going?" he said.

Aharon was too busy chugging water to answer.

It happened so fast, Aharon didn't realize what was going on until it was over. There was a sickening *thud*, and Pini made a strangled sound and crumpled to the ground. Aharon felt himself shoved bodily to the ground; Mohammad was on top of him, shouting. Aharon struggled, trying frantically to free himself. He managed to twist partway around, and from beneath Mohammad's arm he saw that Yusuf was standing over them, holding Aharon's garden shears and shouting back at Mohammad. The garden shears were dripping with blood.

A gunshot cracked the air and Yusuf fell to his knees. Another shot, and Aharon felt Mohammad's full weight crushing down on him. Ears ringing, he fought his way out from beneath Mohammad and scrambled to his feet. Pini was lying on his stomach in the dirt, his rifle still pointing at Mohammad. He peered up at Aharon wild-eyed; then his rifle sank to the ground, and his head followed it, face forward, into the sand.

Aharon heard a shout from the greenhouse and Moshe burst through the doors, pistol drawn. "What the hell happened?!"

Aharon stared down at the three unconscious, bleeding men on the ground.

Moshe cursed in several languages, rushing toward Pini, who lay very still.

"This is what I get for hiring Arab labor..." He was muttering through his teeth, stripping off the soldier's shirt to examine his wounds. "Never again. Never again. Are you all right?" He tossed this last question at Aharon.

"I…" Aharon peered down at the bloodstains on his body, not sure whether any of the blood was his own.

He heard a groan from Mohammad and turned toward him. Blood was gushing from the wound in Mohammad's chest, and red trickles streamed from the corners of his mouth.

Then Aharon spoke aloud what he'd just realized: "Mohammad — he was trying to stop Yusuf from stabbing me too."

Aharon crouched down at Mohammad's side and took his hand. The Arab's eyes flickered open and wandered until they met Aharon's.

"*Shukran, ya khali,*" Aharon thanked him softly.

Mohammad's hand tightened in Aharon's slightly, and their eyes remained locked for a few more moments. Then his grip relaxed, and the light in his eyes faded out.

SACRIFICES

Spring 2001 / Winter 2003

When Rabbi Shlomo and Yossi got home from evening prayers on May 5th, 2001, Shulamit was scurrying around the kitchen in a frenzy, wiping counters, washing pots, putting away dishes, and arranging platters of fruit and cookies.

"But why does he have to come *here?*" she was muttering.

"Relax, relax, woman," Shlomo said, setting down his prayer book on the dining room table and walking over to the kitchen. "He'll only be here for a few minutes before we bring him to the synagogue. He can't possibly eat that much in such a short amount of time."

Shulamit gave him a stern look over her new reading glasses. "Have you seen the man?"

"Shulamit!"

"It's not just him, it's his whole cadre of bodyguards and security personnel…"

"My love, I assure you that they will not touch a single thing you offer them."

"But also Batya…"

"*Now* you're worried about impressing Batya?"

"Oof, Shlomo, just let me work out my nerves the only way I know how." She began rearranging the dates on one of the platters. "It's not every day that the prime minister drops in for a visit."

"Well, let me make *Havdalah* and then you can continue going nuts. Where's Orit?"

"Still napping."

"Yossi, will you wake her?"

"Oof, Abba," the thirteen-year-old whined. His voice was just beginning to break.

"Please, Yossi."

Yossi slouched off down the hallway to wake his sister as Shlomo and Shulamit took down the three-wicked candle, the spices, and the wine goblet. Once sixteen-year-old Orit emerged, bleary-eyed, from the hall, Shulamit mumbled a quick *"Baruch haMavdil"* and turned out the lights, and Shlomo performed a rather hurried rendition of the ceremony for the closing of the Sabbath. As soon as he put out the flame, Shulamit jumped up and went back to her platters.

"Do I have to be here while Sharon is here?" Orit yawned.

"No one's going to tie you to the chair," Shulamit tossed behind her shoulder, "but I think you'll regret missing the opportunity, honey."

"I don't have anything to wear."

"This isn't Cinderella's ball. Just put on something clean."

Shlomo sensed another argument about Orit's wardrobe coming on and took his leave, walking into the living room and opening the curtains of the big bay window. The moon was almost full, and it reflected its pearly white light off the sea. They'd been living in this house for five years, and he never grew tired of the view. The place had felt emptier in the last year; Vered had gotten married and moved to Jerusalem, where she was attending university, and Reut was studying in a seminary in Safed. Orit had followed her sisters to the high school in Dolev, and Yossi had just started attending the yeshiva high school in Yad Binyamin that September, so they were both off in dormitories during the week. Though Rabbi Shlomo had known, theoretically, that his children would probably be attending boarding schools, it hadn't occurred to him that he'd be an empty-nester quite so soon. But he was glad they had built enough rooms for all the children. With God's help, there would soon be grandchildren to host on weekends.

Batya Karni, head of the settlement council, turned up twenty minutes early to help Shulamit set up, and the two of them chatted in breathless voices while Yossi and Orit bickered over the computer. Seven-thirty came and went; it was only half an hour later than planned that the knock came at the door.

"Good evening," Shlomo greeted the security personnel, and stepped back as they secured the building. When they had cleared all the rooms, they nodded to the guards around one of the armored vehicles parked in the Toledanos' driveway, and one of them opened the door. Ariel Sharon stepped out.

"Shalom, honorable prime minister," Rabbi Shlomo said, extending his hand.

"Shalom, honorable rabbi," Sharon responded, giving Shlomo's hand a generous shake. "Shalom shalom," he nodded at the others, who stood nervously a few paces back.

"My wife, Shulamit," Shlomo gestured to her, "and Batya Karni, head of the regional council. These are my children, Orit and Yossi." Sharon extended a hand to Yossi, who shook it, looking dazed.

"We can't tell you how much we appreciate your visit, sir," Batya spoke up. "I can't speak for the others in this room, but know that you had both my vote and my husband's."

"It's my pleasure and my great responsibility," Sharon replied in his throaty voice. "You in Gush Katif have been holding the front lines of the conflict. I intend to do everything I can to ensure your security here."

"Barak's idea of ensuring security seemed to be handing our homes to our enemies," Batya went on, her eyes flashing. "We trust you to have better judgment."

"I had a heavy hand in planning the establishment of this settlement bloc. I assure you I have no intention of dismantling it for any reason."

Rabbi Shlomo accompanied Sharon to his armchair and invited him to sit. Shulamit offered him coffee, but he declined.

"Rabbi Shlomo Toledano." Sharon gave him a smile. "I understand you were injured in Lebanon."

Rabbi Shlomo nodded.

"I must apologize," Sharon said, and Shlomo noticed the weariness in the sagging wrinkles of his face. "I sent you in there."

"It was an honor and privilege, sir."

"How's the leg?"

"*Baruch* Hashem. One day at a time."

"And you?" Sharon addressed the kids. "Where do you go to school?"

The teens both answered in barely audible voices.

"Studying hard?"

They both nodded.

"How have things been here in Neve Adva since the intifada started?"

The residents of Neve Adva exchanged dark glances.

"I have never said the traveler's prayer with as much concentration as I say it whenever I get in the car these days," Batya said, "and every time any one of us arrives home safely, I feel like I should make the *gomel* blessing to thank God for sparing their life."

Shlomo gave a wry nod in agreement. "We should have a marathon of that blessing for every adult in the *yishuv* Mondays,

Thursdays, and Shabbatot. There are very few of us who haven't encountered a rock in the windshield or just barely escaped a shooting attack."

"It's a miracle no one from Neve Adva has been seriously hurt," Shulamit added. "But it's terrifying to send my children anywhere. My daughter was just one block away from the French Hill bombing a month ago. It's miraculous nothing serious has happened from all the mortar shells either."

"There was that incident with Aharon, where the soldier was killed..." said Batya.

"But that was before this stuff started, not that the dates matter. And Aharon surviving that maniac was another miracle," said Shulamit.

"The guardian of Israel neither slumbers nor sleeps," Sharon quoted the book of Psalms. "And neither do I, to be honest." He gave his breathy chortle. "You've done wonderful work with this *yishuv*."

"Thanks to you, sir," said Batya.

"The synagogue is ready, Mr. Prime Minister," one of the bodyguards announced.

The women moved to stand up, but Arik Sharon reached out and lay a gentle hand on Rabbi Shlomo's knee, where the stump met the prosthetic.

"I want to thank you," he said, "for all the sacrifices you have made for the people of Israel."

A rush of emotion flooded through Rabbi Shlomo. He swallowed and replied: "The same to you, sir."

———※———

Their mysterious luck held out until December 9th, 2003.

Shlomo was in his armchair facing his beloved bay window,

bent over a Gemara, when he heard the explosion. He froze for a moment — and went back to studying. It was not unusual to hear bangs and booms in Gush Katif; the Palestinians in Khan Yunis shot missiles and mortars at the Israeli settlements on a near-daily basis during the Second Intifada, and aside from the gun battles between the terrorist group *du jour* and the IDF, Palestinians had an infuriating habit of celebrating everything from weddings to high school exam results with fireworks and gunfire. This one did sound louder and closer than usual, but not alarmingly so. Two minutes later, however, his cellphone buzzed. It was a message from Batya.

Mortar shot at greenhouse. There's a casualty. My office ASAP.

———— ✺ ————

It wasn't that Shulamit hadn't been aware that something like this might happen. It hung over her head from the moment she opened her eyes every morning until the moment she drifted off to sleep — usually after a great deal of tossing and turning. Every time she got in the car to drive to work in Be'er Sheva, she paused for a moment, staring straight ahead at the beach beyond the driveway and gripping the wheel tight, the possible scenarios flashing through her mind. Yet somehow, all her dark imaginings of much worse, much closer incidents still hadn't prepared her for the full force of the news that her neighbor, Aharon Cohen — the guest at their first Shabbat dinner in Neve Adva, the groom at the first wedding there, the man who survived the only other terror attack there — was dead.

The dark imaginings never did help. They didn't help twenty-one years ago, either. She'd been a young mother, only twenty-three, with a two-year-old and a baby on the way, and she'd been through all the scenarios over and over in her mind; and still, nothing had prepared her for the phone call from the army that Shlomo was being helicoptered in to Rambam Hospital in Haifa and his life was hanging by a thread. She dropped Vered off with her parents in Alon Shvut and drove up north, breaking down at every red light and pulling herself together when it turned green.

"Hashem, Hashem, please don't take him," she begged over and over as she clutched the wheel. The drive was three hours long and it was nightfall before she arrived. He'd been injured in a bloody battle and the hospital was in chaos. It took a while for her to find him in the ICU — and longer for her to really be sure it was him underneath all the tubes. She reached out, trembling, to take his hand. It was warm. She sank into a chair next to the bed and closed her eyes, holding that hand in both of hers, listening to the sound of his pulse on the monitor.

"Shulamit." His voice came to her out of a fog. "Did you hear me?"

Shulamit blinked and snapped back to the reality that she was standing in the hallway of the hospital with medical staff jostling past her, not as a visitor, but as a nurse; and that it was Shlomo's voice on the phone, and that it wasn't him, it wasn't him that was hurt this time.

"Aharon?" She didn't recognize her own voice. "Aharon Cohen?"

"We're trying to arrange the funeral for this afternoon. Talia was just notified and the children were sent home. Will you tell the kids?"

Shulamit slumped against the wall behind her, unable to speak.

"Shulamit?"

"I'll tell them, I'll tell them," she said.

"Are you coming?"

"I...I'll have to ask Rina..."

"Are you okay?"

"No. I'm not. I'm really not."

By this time, a few of Shulamit's colleagues had noticed her posture and expression and were exchanging glances, mouthing that word that had become so familiar to all of them in the past three years: *piguah*? Terror attack?

"Me neither." His voice cracked a little. "Be strong, my love. I'll see you soon."

As soon as Shulamit hung up, her colleagues pounced on her:

"What happened, Shulamit?"

"Is everything okay?"

"Who? Where?"

"Oh…in Gush Katif?"

"Do you need us to cover for you? There are only two hours left on your shift, I'm sure Rina will understand."

Shulamit picked up a hitchhiker on her way out of Be'er Sheva — a young woman on her way to the seminary in Neve Dekalim — and turned on the radio to listen for news of Aharon's murder. Aside from a passing mention on Galei Tzahal, no one was talking about it. Shulamit gritted her teeth, feeling a wave of anger.

"I don't get it," she muttered to her passenger. "Is it the body count that makes it matter? Is it the location? If the mortar killed somebody's neighbor in Netivot or Be'er Sheva would it be all over the news? Or does it have to be three casualties or more before people start to care?"

"The blood of Jewish settlers is cheap," the girl said bitterly.

One week later, Talia and the children rose from the *shiva*, and Shlomo and Shulamit joined the rest of the community in accompanying them for their first walk around the neighborhood.

Shulamit put Aharon's children to bed while Shlomo sat with Talia to discuss her finances and figure out what she would need from the community in the coming months. They arrived home around nine, bone-tired, and sank onto the couch. Shlomo switched on the television. Ariel Sharon appeared on the screen.

"If, in the coming months, the Palestinians do not uphold their part in the Road Map," he was saying, "Israel will then initiate a unilateral process of disengagement from the Palestinians."

"In a surprising change of policy," the newscaster explained, "Prime Minister Ariel Sharon today announced a plan to unilaterally evacuate certain Israeli settlements beyond the Green Line if the current round of peace talks fails. Details of this plan have yet to be made public, but there is conjecture that…"

Shlomo and Shulamit sat side by side, staring numbly at the screen as the newscaster prattled on.

TWO CAN PLAY

Winter 2004

Olga Borokhov waited until her twin sister's silhouette disappeared from her kitchen window before stepping out of the car. Bathed in the yellowish light of the streetlamp, she made her way to her own front door and opened it gently. She unpinned her nametag and tossed it into the dish on the little table by the entranceway that was designated for holding such odds and ends. Then she hung her coat and purse and turned toward the living room.

Baruch was facing away from her, with the television blaring in front of him, and she could tell by the tilt of his shaven head and the way it rose and fell gently with his breath that he was sleeping. Her eyes swept the house, her lips tightening as she noticed the scraps of omelet still scattered on and under the table. She tiptoed to the kids' room and cracked the door open, watching their chests rise and fall for a few cycles of breath before returning to clean up the scraps of dinner.

When she had swept and scrubbed the table and its surroundings to her satisfaction, she sat down next to Baruch on the couch, eyes narrowing at the screen. It was a political commentary show, and they were talking about Sharon's recently announced plans to pull out of the territories. There were four men sitting around a table in the studio, and they were all talking on top of each other in Hebrew too rapid for Olga to understand. She felt her jaw clench tighter and tighter as she watched.

Baruch stirred, and reached out for Olga's hand.

"Baruch," Olga said.

"Mm."

"We should leave."

Baruch rolled his head over to look at her, and they studied each other carefully.

Then Baruch sighed and cast his eyes on the floor.

"Even if this plan doesn't pass," Olga went on, "there will be another, and another. I can't stand the uncertainty. It's not good for the kids, either. I want to move someplace else."

Baruch was casting a slow, wistful gaze over the walls he had built with his own hands.

"I know," Olga said.

He turned to look at her again.

"What about Mickey and Svetka?" His voice was a low whisper, as if their cousin and sister could hear them through the walls.

Olga stared ahead at the screen again and didn't answer.

The next week, Olga kept the kids home from school, Baruch made some excuse to leave Mickey to the fishing on his own, and they piled into the car and began the drive north along the coast. Baruch turned into a city here, a town there, but after a few circles, Olga would shake her head and they would turn back onto the highway.

"Where are we even going?" Binyamin whined from the back seat after three hours of this, when they were already approaching Haifa.

"They don't know." Kinneret cast her best disgusted-preteen scowl at her parents through the rearview mirror. "They're just going to keep driving until we get to Lebanon."

She wasn't far off the mark. It was only when the cliffs of Rosh HaNikra loomed ahead that Olga suddenly said, "Pull over. There, by the beach."

The five of them spilled out of the car, and Olga made her way across the sand toward the seamline between the sea and the rocks. Heavy storm clouds hung close to the mountains above, and the sea was frothy and slate-gray. The wind whipped Olga's straight strawberry-blond hair around her ears as she scanned the line where the sky met the sea.

Baruch squinted up at the cliff jutting up out of the water up ahead, his eyes resting on the IDF flag planted on top.

"I think we've run out of coastline," he said.

"This is the place."

Baruch furrowed his brow at Olga.

"What? Here?"

"What's the nearest village?"

Back in the car, they consulted a map. The nearest village was a tiny rural town named Betzet. They spotted a "For Sale" sign on a cozy little cottage tucked among the eucalyptus trees. It was small, only three bedrooms, and Kinneret and Benny started bickering about who should get their own room, but Olga shot them a look and they clamped their mouths shut. She and Baruch signed the contract then and there and headed back down to Nahariya to find a place to eat a late lunch.

Until Binyamin's birth, Svetka had been the first to know about everything — from Olga's crush on that dark-haired Jewish boy in their second-grade class in Moscow to the first time she woke in the middle of the night with bloody underwear. They'd been inducted into the IDF on the same day and served in the same unit in the optics corps, fixing night vision goggles by day and passing off boys — who couldn't tell them apart, but didn't seem to care one way or the other — by night.

When Olga met Baruch in the design program at Hadassah College, he was quick to introduce Svetka to his cousin Mickey, and they'd gotten married within three months of each other and moved down to Dugit and then Neve Adva together. When Olga had Kinneret, Svetka knew first about every tiny milestone.

After Svetka's miscarriage, though, Olga found herself faltering, asking herself whether it was really worth mentioning that Benny had started crawling, or had managed to break into the pantry and scatter rice all over the floor, or that Kinneret had started refusing to speak to her in Russian, or had taught herself to read in kindergarten. She felt these subjects bubble up in her, but then she would pause. Would it be worth the emptiness in Svetka's face, the pain in her eyes, the twitch in her lips when she didn't respond? More and more, Olga chose to swallow the words. She waited three months to tell anyone except Baruch about her pregnancy with Levana, and when she did finally tell Svetka, Svetka's lips went tight and her eyes were glued to the floor as she said in a quiet voice, "I was wondering when you were going to tell me." And then, with what seemed like monumental effort, she pulled the corners of her lips into something resembling a smile and kissed her sister on the cheeks.

"*Mazal tov*, Olga," she'd said, and somehow her efforts to express happiness were more painful to Olga than the sorrow that she knew was underneath.

The kids grew up moving freely between Olga's house and Svetka's, and sometimes when Olga caught the softness in

Svetka's eyes as she read a storybook to Levana or served Binyamin another helping of her famous fish in cream sauce, she would wonder if the tension was behind them. But by then, maintaining the silence had become easier than breaching it.

The matter of moving would be a delicate one. Svetka had developed a habit of spitting on the floor whenever Ariel Sharon's name was mentioned in conversation. She astonished Olga by getting involved with the Mateh Hamaavak, the political organization formed to fight the disengagement plan — not the type of activity Olga normally associated with her shy, soft-spoken twin. Svetka further astonished her by snapping at Baruch when he casually threw out the concept of selling their fishing business so they could move somewhere else if necessary over dinner one night — saying sharply that it would never be necessary and he shouldn't even mention such things. Olga couldn't remember the last time she'd heard Svetka speak harshly to anyone.

But Olga knew she would have to tell Svetka eventually; the sisters had never lived apart, not for a single day. For weeks after signing the contract in Betzet, she kept planning to bring it up, but since taking that job at the medical clinic in Neve Dekalim, her hours were all out of sync with Svetka's and it seemed impossible to find the right moment.

"It isn't right," Baruch blurted out to her late one Friday night after Mickey and Svetka had gone home and Olga was somehow finishing off the last slice of strawberry layer cake while loading the dishwasher. "I can't withhold it from Mickey anymore, Olga. We have to talk about what to do with the business. I can't just disappear one day and expect him to manage it by himself."

"I know, I know."

"Why don't you just *tell* her?"

"I've been trying!" Olga snapped.

Baruch threw up his hands and sank onto the couch, but said no more. Olga glared at the back of his shaven head, collecting the last of the cream on her plate with her finger and licking it off before shoving the plate in the dishwasher and slamming it closed. She walked around the table toward the couch and sat down next to him.

"The potential buyers are coming to see the place on Sunday," he said. "Are you going to sneak them in the back door? You have to tell her, Olga, before she finds out herself."

———

But all through Saturday no opportunity presented itself. Olga spent a major portion of the day scrubbing floors until they shined and snapping at the kids to organize their shelves. Svetka dropped in briefly to borrow some sugar, but she didn't linger when she saw that Olga was on one of her cleaning rampages. Baruch cast many meaningful looks at Olga whenever she was sitting still, at which point she always remembered something else she'd forgotten to do.

Olga arranged an earlier shift for Sunday so she could show the house to the potential buyers. She'd been shocked at how much interest the house had gotten once they'd put it on the market. Who would be interested in moving somewhere that would probably be evacuated by the government soon? Many, apparently. Svetka had mentioned something about an effort to strengthen the "demographic impact" of the place. Olga hadn't said anything at the time, but she had thought that it was one thing to do that as politically active adults, and another thing entirely to bring children into Gaza as political pawns in a losing game. It was bad enough watching her children get on buses that would take them on these deadly roads to school.

In fact, the truth was that Olga was never entirely happy about living in Neve Adva. She didn't mind the isolation; she was a woman of simple needs. It was the crushing sense of danger. Every time she was outside when the sun sank just below the horizon and the muezzins called the Muslims to prayer in the neighboring villages — all grainy recordings of the same voice, and all slightly out of sync, creating an ominous cacophony blasting from multiple directions — the hairs on the back of her neck stood on end. Whenever she drove past Kissufim Checkpoint on her way into Israel proper, her lungs seemed to expand to twice their previous capacity.

And then there was the incident with Aharon. She'd been casual friends with Talia Cohen before Aharon's death, but afterwards Olga could not bring herself to look Talia in the eye anymore. She was afraid she would burst into tears every time she saw her face. So she found herself avoiding Talia. She knew it was cruel, but she simply could not withstand the reminder of how close they were to the maw of the abyss.

For weeks, maybe months after Aharon's death, Levana came into Olga's room in the middle of the night, whimpering about nightmares with bad guys and bombs trying to kill her. After Olga would calm her, she refused to go back to her bed, sobbing that she was afraid the nightmares would come back. Olga would shush her and stroke her hair, and then lie awake long after her child's body became heavy and her breath slow and rhythmic. She would hold Levana tight, helpless against the tears dripping onto her pillow because she could neither promise her daughter that the nightmares wouldn't return, nor that they wouldn't come true.

Property was cheap in Gush Katif, though, and Mickey and Baruch had established a lucrative business after learning the trade in Dugit. The house they were buying in Betzet was much smaller than the one in Neve Adva, and while she'd been cleaning on Saturday, as she'd scrubbed the marble mantle of the fireplace Baruch had designed and built himself, a tear that wasn't from cleaning-chemical fumes escaped down her cheek.

<hr>

The Zaguris were supposed to come by around 7 o'clock on Sunday evening. Olga set a plate of cookies on the dining room table and her kids in front of the TV, and waited with her hands folded, glancing at the clock every now and then. At 7:15 she heard a car pulling over near their driveway and doors slamming, but there were no footsteps approaching her door, so she figured maybe her sister had visitors and allowed herself to be distracted by the movie her kids were watching.

A few minutes later there was a knock on the door, and Olga sprang up to open it. A Middle Eastern middle-aged couple stood on her doorstep looking perplexed — and Svetka was standing behind them, her lips in a tight line and her brow deeply furrowed. Olga felt her stomach drop at the sight of her sister.

"Are you Olga?" the Zaguri woman asked.

"Yes," Olga replied, feeling her mouth go dry.

"These people," Svetka spoke up from behind them in her heavily accented Hebrew, "came to our house and seemed to think we were putting it up for sale. When I told them I had no intention of ever selling our house, they said they had spoken to Olga Borokhov about the purchase, and had thought it was ours because of the sign that says 'Borokhov' on our door. I told them they had to be mistaken, because there is no way on earth the Olga Borokhov I know could be selling her house."

Olga swallowed, feeling her hands trembling. She took a deep breath.

"Svetka, please," she said quietly in Russian, "go home and we will talk about this later."

"We will not talk about this later!" Svetka's eyes were bulging out of her head, her face turning a bright shade of red. The Zaguris exchanged uncomfortable glances.

"Svetka." Olga's voice grew sharp. "Please."

Mrs. Zaguri cleared her throat.

"Perhaps we should come another time..." she said.

"No, no, please come in," Olga said, and they stepped into the house. "Later," she said to Svetka, and shut the door in her sister's livid face.

Olga gave the Zaguris a tour of the house, and they followed her in stiff, polite silence, casting worried glances at the door every so often.

"Well, it's a lovely place," said Mrs. Zaguri when they had returned to the dining area near the entrance. "We'll be in touch."

"I hope we didn't cause you too much trouble with...ah...your neighbor," said Mr. Zaguri.

"Oh, never mind her," Olga said, but she was not very good at faking nonchalance, and the Zaguris exchanged one last concerned look before opening the door to leave. There was no sign of Svetka, and they all breathed a sigh of relief and bid farewell. Olga shut the door behind them and closed her eyes, leaning her forehead forward onto the door and resting there for a few minutes. When she pulled herself together and stood up, Baruch was standing opposite her with his arms crossed and an accusing I-told-you-so glare.

"Don't," Olga snapped at him, before pulling the door back open and stepping out into the night.

Olga stood on Svetka's doorstep for a minute or two before bringing herself to knock. The door did not open. The curtains were drawn on the living room window, but there was light filtering through them. She knocked again.

"Svetka," she called. "Please open the door."

No answer. Olga sidled over to the living room window and squinted through the red cotton gauze of the curtains. She could just make out an outline of a figure sitting on the white leather couch.

"Svetka," she called, rapping on the window. "Svetka, are you there? Please let me explain."

When this didn't yield any results either, Olga stepped back, swallowing a wave of nausea and fighting back tears. She set her jaw.

"Fine," she whispered. "Fine."

***

Olga did not see Svetka the next morning when she was herding the kids out to school. On her way back, she paused at the end of Svetka's driveway, but made her way back to her house and fixed herself a strong cup of tea. Baruch was still sitting at the table with his coffee, shirtless, the Star of David necklace he always wore under his clothes glinting in the light streaming in from the kitchen window. They sat and sipped in silence.

"You should go speak to Mickey," Olga said, squeezing her teabag into her empty cup.

"I'm sure she'll speak to you today," said Baruch.

But she didn't. Neither of them saw a trace of Svetka over the next few days. Baruch and Mickey met at the pier they had built together and worked out the details of Baruch's partnership in the business; Olga didn't know how the conversation went, but

Baruch came home earlier and surlier than usual, and didn't make any comments about Mickey's and Svetka's absence throughout the next few days. When Olga caught Svetka tending her flowers in the front garden one morning, she tried to approach her, but Svetka quickly disappeared into the house. Olga entertained the question of whether she should follow and try to appease her, but she felt a flare of anger at the thought of it and set her jaw, marching back inside her house.

Olga found herself practicing their confrontation in her bathroom mirror every night after brushing her teeth. She would look deep into the icy green eyes of her reflection — identical to those of her sister — and find herself talking about everything, not only the imminent move, but all the silences of the past nine years, all the things Olga had been afraid to say and to ask, all the issues with Olga's kids that had been tiptoed around, and the birth, Benny's birth, the birth that Svetka had never once asked or spoken about. Olga would find herself crying, and she would wash her face furiously before leaving the bathroom and going to bed.

Within a week or so, Olga noticed the other members of the yishuv murmuring and their gazes lingering on her as she passed them in the street. Soon, mutual friends were approaching her in hushed voices to ask what was going on between her and her sister. Olga would tell them matter-of-factly that she and Baruch were leaving and Svetka didn't take it well, and they would nod sympathetically and move on. Shulamit, the rabbi's wife, told her that she was trying to encourage Svetka to speak to Olga and hear her side, but nothing ever came of it.

Over time, Olga's bathroom-mirror conversations hardened from pleading and begging to sharp accusation. "*You drove me away*," she found herself hissing at her reflection. And she no longer searched the living room window for Svetka's silhouette, no longer let her eyes linger on Svetka's doorstep as she walked past in the mornings. When her friends asked her if anything had changed with Svetka she would ignore the question and change the subject. "Two can play at this game," she growled at her reflection in the bathroom mirror.

And when they pulled out of the driveway to follow the moving truck that spring, Olga kept her eyes on the road ahead of them, her jaw square, softening only when Baruch reached out to give her hand a gentle squeeze.

ASCENSION

Summer 2004

The wheels of the plane lost contact with the earth, and despite the heaviness of his one-year-old daughter's sleeping body on his lap, Reuben felt weightless. The passengers around him were clapping and singing *"Am Yisrael Chai"* — "The Nation of Israel Lives" — and as they ascended toward the clouds and the buildings of New York City shrunk to toy size below them, the excitement quieted to reverent hush. Shelly slipped her hand into Reuben's, and he peeked around Shira's pigtails to beam at his wife. There were tears in her eyes, and she blinked and looked away. He couldn't tell if they were tears of sadness or joy. Probably a mixture of both.

The last time Reuben had boarded a plane to Israel, he'd sported a Guns N' Roses T-shirt and ripped jeans, anticipating ten days of partying and drinking. Now he wore a practical button-down shirt and a kippah on his head, and while the plane was boarding, his mind had been full of patently adult worries, like whether he'd remembered to bring all the documents in the checklist, and whether the HMO he'd selected to provide health insurance would be the best choice for the area they were moving to. He'd caught snippets of conversation around them discussing the same things; it was a charter flight through Nefesh B'Nefesh, an organization that helped Jews make aliyah, and everyone else on the plane was a new immigrant like him.

Shira stirred in Reuben's lap and emitted a whimper and then a wail. Shelly reached for her, pulling out her nursing cover, and Reuben passed the baby over, grateful for the reprieve. He watched Shelly arrange herself to calm Shira, and then lean back, tucking a stray curl back beneath her beret. He felt a wave of nostalgia; their first conversation about aliyah had been on their first date. They were both studying at Boston University and were set up by a mutual friend. After a few minutes of exchanging pleasantries and scanning the menu, Shelly informed him that aliyah was a make-or-break issue for her.

"I'm going to finish my degree, but as soon as I've graduated, I'm going to Israel," she had told him.

Up until that point, he hadn't thought very seriously about moving to Israel. The Hillel organization on campus had opened his eyes to the beauty of Jewish tradition, much to the chagrin of his fervently Reform parents; only a few months earlier, he'd had to inform his mother that he could no longer eat in her kitchen, and it sparked a major family crisis. He had one sister who wasn't speaking to him anymore, and several cousins who had been chilly toward him ever since. He had imagined the look on his mother's face if he'd had to tell her that he was going to move halfway across the world. But something mesmerized him about Shelly's earnest brown eyes and firm confidence, and he told her that he was open to the possibility.

Of course, things never quite work out as planned. Reuben and Shelly decided to get married a few months later, and Shelly was pregnant with Daniel at her graduation ceremony. Reuben decided to go for his MBA, and Shelly got a stable job at a speech therapy clinic in the city, and they decided that maybe it would be better to wait until they had saved up a little.

To the bewilderment of all their relatives, it was the Café Hillel bombing in September of 2003 that spurred them to move forward with their plans. Reuben found Shelly crying in front of the TV. She sobbed about Nava Applebaum, the young bride who had been killed the night before her wedding, and missed opportunities, and how life was too short to keep putting off their dream of establishing their rightful place in the world.

"We have to go," Shelly had said, clutching his hands, her eyes wide and bloodshot. "We have to go. As revenge."

Reuben had been slowly preparing his mother for this news since his courtship with Shelly, but nonetheless, the look on her face when he told her they'd signed up to be aboard the July 2004 charter flight shattered him.

"Are you crazy?" she'd moaned. "Now?! Now of all times?! How could you deliberately choose to put your children in that kind of danger? How can you take my grandchildren away to get blown up by a terrorist?"

"That kind of thinking is what lets terror win," he'd said, trying not to sound defensive. "They're far more likely to be killed in a car accident..."

His mother was not interested in statistics. Even when she'd bid them goodbye at Logan Airport, she had whispered to him that he could always come back if it didn't work out. He'd had to clamp his lips together. She had thought "the religious thing" was just a phase, too.

"Abba, are you mad?"

The voice of his six-year-old pulled him out of his reverie, and he glanced, startled, at the child sitting next to him on the plane. Then his face relaxed into a smile.

"No, sweetheart. Just thinking."

"Is Pizza Hut really kosher in Israel?" Daniel asked for the thousandth time.

"Yep."

"Can we go there when we get there?"

Reuben reached out and ran a hand through his son's hair. "You bet."

The plane shuddered, rattling the fold-up trays in front of them, and Daniel clutched his dad's arm, his eyes wide.

"Abba, is the plane going to break?"

"No, sweetheart. It's just turbulence. It's what happens when the plane hits some rough air currents. It's normal, and it'll stop soon."

He wasn't sure even he understood what that meant, but he patted his son's hand, and Daniel's grip on his arm slackened.

Reuben leaned back and closed his eyes as the plane rocked him in his seat. He found a little turbulence more reassuring than the usual stillness of flight. Erratic movement seemed more consistent with the reality of hurtling through the atmosphere in a large metal tube, 30,000 feet off the ground.

Several hours later, Reuben found himself stumbling through the aisles in the dark, trying to keep up with Shira and prevent her from disturbing the other passengers. He hadn't remembered the flight being quite this long, but then again, the only time he'd been to Israel was on Birthright, and that time he didn't have any rambunctious toddlers to chase after. He exchanged tired smiles with the other parents pouring juice for their own kids in the back of the plane, and eavesdropped on snippets of their conversations:

"Where to?"

"Be'er Sheva. You?"

"Netzer Hazani."

"Oh, really? In Gaza? That's gutsy."

"As if it makes much of a difference these days."

Reuben exchanged a furtive look of solidarity with the guy heading for Be'er Sheva. It was one thing moving to Israel despite all the suicide bombings. It was another thing entirely to plant yourself right in the middle of all the angriest Palestinians. Shelly might have considered living beyond the Green Line — probably someplace a little more sane than Gaza, like Efrat in Gush Etzion — but when they sat down to discuss potential locations, she saw the look on his face as soon as she mentioned it, and slid her finger across the map to the central region of Israel. They chose Rehovot, a quiet little city south of Tel Aviv and not far from the coast, which, he was told, had decent schools and a significant community of religious English-speakers.

When the lights came on and the smells of breakfast wafted through the air, a murmur of excitement swept through the cabin. They were only two hours away. Reuben was groggy from the hour or two of sleep he'd managed to catch while Shelly took the Shira shift, but began glancing at the flight map depicting the European coasts drifting by below them, feeling an electricity flowing through him. *Almost there. Almost there.*

Finally, the wheels of the plane touched the ground. The passengers burst into an uproar of applause, cheering, singing, and clapping.

"We are proud and honored to be the first to welcome you all home to Israel," said the captain over the loudspeaker.

"We're here, we're here!" Daniel squealed, and Shelly squeezed Reuben's hand. Her eyes were watery again.

The flight crew joined in an emotional rendition of Hatikva as the plane taxied toward the gate. The new *olim* pulled out the Israeli flags that had been passed out at JFK, gathered their belongings, and filed toward the door. Reuben felt a blast of hot, humid air as he neared the entrance and stepped out into the brilliant sun. He shuffled down the stairs, blinking as his eyes adjusted to the light, and felt himself trembling as he drew closer to the ground. When his feet finally connected with the land his ancestors dreamed of for two thousand years, he dropped to his knees, bent down, and kissed the ground. Eyes filling with tears, he turned to Shelly — who was carrying Shira on her hip — and Daniel as they stepped down onto the tarmac themselves.

"Welcome home, Shelly," said Reuben in a choked voice.

"Welcome home, welcome home!" Shelly threw her free arm around Reuben, and Daniel rushed in to join the family hug, and Shelly's rolling laugh carried over the hubbub of the crowd.

Reuben had rented a fully furnished temporary apartment for the first three months while they waited for the lift with all their furniture to arrive. It was located a few blocks away from their new house in a squat apartment building covered in ugly brown stucco. There was a large sign hanging from one of the windows with what seemed like a political slogan. Reuben squinted at it, trying to read. The first and last words were the same: *yehudi*, which, he knew, means "Jew". The second word was *lo*, which means "no"; but what was the third word? *Magrash? Magresh? Migrash?*

"See the palm trees in the yard?" Shelly was pointing with one hand on Daniel's arm. He stared up at them in awe.

There was no elevator, which made getting the stroller up a bit of a chore. Shelly stayed upstairs with the kids while Reuben lugged the suitcases up one by one. She handed him a glass of cold water as he collapsed onto the sagging couch in the living room and took in his surroundings. Everything felt so small: the little table tucked into the corner of the living room, the three feet of counter space next to the sink in the kitchen, the narrow beds, the strange toilet bowl with the tiny pool of water at the bottom. Shelly set up Shira's Pack 'n Play while Reuben worked on fulfilling his promise to Daniel: there was a kosher Pizza Hut across town. Eager to try out his Hebrew, Reuben dialed the restaurant, but before he'd gotten three words out, the man at the other end switched to heavily accented English.

"Oh, gosh," Shelly gushed as she opened the pizza box and the aroma wafted through the living room. "Welcome to the Promised Land!" She had grown up in an observant family, so for her and Daniel, eating at ordinary places like Pizza Hut and McDonald's was a novelty. Reuben, who had started keeping kosher only shortly before he met Shelly, was far less enchanted by the greasy pizza, but enjoyed watching the delight on the faces of his wife and son as they scarfed it down.

The sun was setting, and Reuben felt heavy with exhaustion. Shelly took the kids into their room to begin the bedtime routine, and ten minutes later, Reuben tiptoed into the room to find all three of them asleep — Daniel tucked into bed, Shira curled up in her Pack 'n Play, and Shelly sprawled out on the floor. He went into the master bedroom and tiptoed around the bed, which took up most of the floor space in the room, and found a blanket in the wardrobe. He carried it back into the kids' room and spread the blanket gently over his wife, pausing for a moment to listen to the sound of their breathing. The place was different, cramped; the floors were hard, unforgiving tile; even the smell was different . . . not unpleasant, but not what he was used to. He knew there would be a lot more than all that to adjust to in the coming days and months. But at least, he thought, they would be doing it together.

The next day the family took a walk to visit the house they had purchased. The air was heavy with heat, but nothing a family from Boston wouldn't be accustomed to. The house was smaller than Reuben had imagined, attached on both sides, with a tiny strip of garden next to the single parking space in front. They ascended the stairs, leaving the stroller in the yard, and Reuben fumbled with the key before managing to unlock and swing the steel door open.

They stepped inside, looking around eagerly. Daniel took off upstairs to find his room. Reuben slowly paced the length and breadth of the house, his footsteps echoing strangely against the concrete walls. On their final walk-through of their home in Boston, he had done the same thing, trying to etch every detail into his memory; but without the furniture, it had felt strangely foreign. Here, instead of carpeting, there was dull white tile; instead of wood flooring, more tile; instead of wallpaper, plain whitewashed walls. The kitchen counters were a pale cream marble, the kitchen cabinets coated in plain white Formica, in contrast to the sturdy maple of their cabinets in Boston. Naked bulbs hung from the ceilings. There was a small laundry balcony on the second floor; Reuben noted they would have to keep that door locked when he saw Daniel attempting to climb on the stone railing. On the bottom floor was their built-in bomb shelter: a room of reinforced concrete with a metal shutter that could be rolled into place outside the window, and rubber seals around the edges of the window and the heavy steel door. Reuben remembered reading about Israelis using duct tape and wet towels to seal their rooms during the first Gulf War; this was certainly an improvement.

"Well?" he prompted Shelly as she descended the stairs, Shira on hip, back into the empty space that would become their living room. She gave him a tired smile.

"I can't wait to see what we'll do with it," she said.

NOT THE WAY

Summer 2004 / Spring 2005

On July 25th, 2004, Yossi Toledano stood on Route 4 with his mother on one side and his father on the other. He bent forward and looked down the human chain, squinting at the point where the row of people shrank into nothingness in the distance. Somewhere down there, many kilometers away, his sister Orit was standing with her friends from national service; and up on Jaffa Street, not far from the Old City of Jerusalem, his sisters Reut and Vered were standing with their husbands and children. Was the chain really unbroken, he wondered? He imagined passing a candy bar down the line to see if it would reach his sisters eventually.

Someone had a radio tuned in to Radio Kol Chai blasting from near the spot where he stood, and when seven o'clock came, he heard the tune of Hatikva drifting toward him from both sides simultaneously — down the human chain, and from the radio behind them. Yossi closed his eyes and held tight to the hands of his parents, plugging in to the connection between his past, his present, and his future; between Gaza and Jerusalem; between the Israelis all along the human spectrum who had come to show their solidarity with Gush Katif and demonstrate that they were all connected, engaged, entangled and intertwined for all eternity.

His eyes filled with tears as he sang at the top of his voice: *Our hope has not yet been lost...the hope of two thousand years...to be a free people in our land, the land of Zion and Jerusalem.*

And he believed, with complete faith, that they would win.

But by May of 2005, things were different.

Yossi coughed as a cloud of thick, acrid smoke plumed from the tire his classmate Gadi had just managed to ignite.

"Back away!" Gadi grabbed Yossi by the arm and pulled him back a few meters to dive back into the crowd gathered at Geha Junction along Route 4. An angry bellow rose from several of the policemen who had been prowling in front of the crowd, trying — rather unsuccessfully — to keep the protesters off the highway.

"Who did that?! Who?!"

The crowd was chanting an incoherent mess of slogans now; every time Yossi tried to join one, it seemed they had transitioned to another. He felt pressure build up behind him, and stumbled forward as a group of protesters burst onto the highway. Traffic was backed up as usual, so no one was going faster than a crawl, and the protesters — mostly teens — spread out in front of the cars in their bright orange T-shirts, banging on the car hoods. Yossi stood in front of a black Honda, peering directly at the driver behind the wheel.

"Wake up, Israelis!" he yelled, waving his arms over his head.

The driver honked furiously, shouting and gesticulating from within the car, but Yossi couldn't hear a word.

"A Jew doesn't expel another Jew!" Yossi's voice broke and he coughed again; his throat stung from the smoke and exhaust.

He felt rough hands grab him by the shoulders, and he was tossed like a trash bag onto the pavement.

"Get up!" A heavy boot connected with his ribcage and he let out a howl of pain. "Get up, get out of the road, you idiot!" Yossi instinctively curled into a ball, protecting his head with his hands. The asphalt beneath him was burning hot. The policeman let out a roar of frustration and lifted the seventeen-year-old forcefully by the shoulders, shoving him into the arms of another officer, who was not any gentler as he seized Yossi in a headlock and dragged him back to the side of the road. There was a bus parked on the shoulder of the highway, and policemen were stuffing it full of young people in orange T-shirts. The policeman who had grabbed Yossi pulled him toward the bus, trying to shove him through the front door. The vehicle was full beyond capacity, and the bus driver was yelling over the crowd that it was illegal for him to drive anywhere under these conditions.

"We are the police!" bellowed Yossi's captor. "You will take all these criminals to Tzidkiyahu; that's an order!" The protesters in front of Yossi fell back a little, pushing him off the front step of the bus. Yossi cried out in pain again as another heavy boot connected with his back. The officer was kicking him back into the bus. The door twisted shut behind him, narrowly avoiding his ankles, and he leaned back against the glass, trying to catch his breath as the bus revved up and started moving.

More than the night he spent in the jail cell with several dozen other young men, more than the criminal charges he knew would be pressed against him for participating in the protest, Yossi was terrified of the look on his father's face when he came to pick him up in the morning. Rabbi Shlomo didn't say a single word to him beyond two-syllable instructions as he led him out to the parking lot, and the first half of the drive back down to Yad Binyamin was spent in tense silence. Yossi waited, biting his lip so hard it bled.

Finally, Rabbi Shlomo opened his mouth.

"I don't know what to do with you, Yossi."

Yossi knew better than to speak now. He stared at his lap, playing absently with the fringes of his *tzitzit*.

"What more can I say? You've heard me say it a thousand times. This is not the way."

"*Your* way doesn't seem to be doing much," Yossi spat, unable to contain himself.

Rabbi Shlomo took a deep breath. "I know it may seem that way to you," he said, his voice shaking a little, as though he were forcing it to remain even. "But burning tires and jumping in front of cars on the highway is the opposite of helpful to our cause. It only increases antagonism, increases the anger, increases the hatred. We don't need any more of that now."

"'We have love and it will win,'" Yossi quoted the slogan in a mocking voice.

Rabbi Shlomo glanced at his son, his jaw hardening. "Is this all some kind of joke to you, Yossi? Do you realize the implications of being charged with disruption of public order? Of deliberately endangering the lives of people? Do you understand what might have happened if a car had caught fire from one of those tires? If someone had been hurt? Do you understand what it looks like when a group of teenagers attacks the car of an innocent Arab, like a mob of barbaric terrorists?"

"We didn't do that."

"You'll have a criminal record now. It may hurt your prospects in the professional world, in the army..."

"As if I want to serve in the army of this country."

Rabbi Shlomo slammed on the brakes, jerking the car to the side of the road, his eyes smoldering.

"Don't...you dare," he hissed. "Don't you dare."

Yossi clamped his lips shut again, looking out the side window at the shrubs in the sand next to the road.

"Look at me," Shlomo said. Yossi shrugged one shoulder. "*Look at me.*" Yossi turned, his jaw set in defiance.

"God did not bring us back to this land after two thousand years to have us reject His gift just because we don't like the policies of the current government. You have no right to turn your back on this country. I don't need to remind you what our family has sacrificed for Israel."

"But was it worth it, Abba?" Yossi fixed his father with a challenging glare. "Everything you fought for in Lebanon — we pulled out of there, too, and it became a breeding ground for Hezbollah. The first few years living in isolation in Neve Adva, the years we had mortars raining down on our roofs, the windshields we had smashed by the rocks and Molotov cocktails from Khan Yunis, our neighbor Aharon...was it all worth it if we're just going to let ourselves be herded out of there like a flock of sheep?"

Rabbi Shlomo sighed, shook his head for a moment, and then started up the car again.

"You don't understand, son," he said. "You don't understand any of it."

Once his father pulled out of the driveway and Yossi set foot back in the Yad Binyamin campus, however, he was an instant hero.

Students he'd never spoken to before pointed and waved at him, and some of the twelfth-graders — who normally turned up their noses at eleventh-graders — clapped him on the back and congratulated him. His teachers said nothing about the protests, but their smiles for him were warm, and when he approached his Gemara teacher about a quiz he had missed, the rabbi waved him off and told him not to worry about it.

Gadi, his roommate, grinned at him when he walked into their dorm room after classes that evening. "Have you seen the papers?" he asked. Yossi shook his head. "We made a big splash, Yossi." Gadi tossed him a copy of *Yediot Aharonot*. Photographs of Route 4 and the burning tires were emblazoned across the front page. "Now they will know once and for all: Gush Katif isn't going down without a fight."

Yossi sank onto the bed, searching the photo to see if he could spot himself.

"How'd it go with your dad?"

Yossi rolled his eyes. "As expected."

Gadi squinted at Yossi's arms. "Is that from yesterday?" he said, pointing to the scratches and bruises.

"That's nothing." Yossi lifted his shirt so Gadi could admire the huge black-and-blue mark over his ribs where the policeman had kicked him.

"Whoa," said Gadi, his eyes wide in appreciation. "That's from the police?"

Yossi nodded.

"Those bastards."

"Are you coming to Rav Eliezer's talk tonight?"

"We have to, don't we?"

"That's what they said," Yossi shrugged.

"How many other students from Yad Binyamin were caught?"

"No idea."

Seventeen, it turned out. They shuffled, one by one, into the classroom where Rav Eliezer waited for them, bent over a Gemara. He didn't look up. Even after they were all seated, sitting silently in a half-circle of chairs arranged in front of the desk, Rav Eliezer did not acknowledge their presence, and they waited.

Finally, without looking up, Rav Eliezer spoke.

"The first Temple..." he said, rocking back and forth over his book, "why was it destroyed?"

The boys exchanged glances.

"Idolatry, sexual immorality, and murder," a gangly twelfth-grader spoke up.

"But the second Temple, in which the Torah was practiced, and the commandments, and charity — why was it destroyed?"

Silence.

Rav Eliezer finally looked up from his Gemara, and his fierce blue eyes gazed straight into Yossi's. Yossi felt a tingle go down his spine.

"Every Jewish child knows the answer," Rav Eliezer said, slamming the Gemara shut.

"Baseless hatred," whispered Yossi.

"Come again?"

"Baseless hatred," he repeated.

"Baseless hatred." Rav Eliezer planted his hands on the desk in front of him and stood, drawing himself up to his full height. "It is no accident," he went on, "that the destruction of Gush Katif is planned for the day after Tisha B'Av, the day we mourn the destruction of both Temples. It seems our young people have not learned anything in the past two thousand years."

"We are not acting out of hatred, honored Rabbi," Gadi spoke up.

Rav Eliezer sighed and began to pace the room. "I know that, Mr. Goldstein. That is why I won't punish you. I know you believe you are acting out of love. I know many of your parents and community leaders support this kind of harsh protest against the disengagement. And I know," he said, stealing a glance at Yossi, "that some of you feel directly threatened by the imminent disaster. It is inspiring to see young people willing to put themselves in harm's way, willing to sit in jail, to put a stop to the atrocity." He clutched the back of his chair and gazed piercingly into the eyes of each student. "But, my dear boys, *this is not the way.*"

Yossi tried not to roll his eyes.

"Perhaps you are not acting out of baseless hatred. But surely you have noticed that baseless hatred is seeping into every crack and corner of our society. The nation of Israel is splitting apart, is disengaging from itself and from one another. Violent protest, burning tires, stopping traffic — these are things that contribute to baseless hatred. They pour fuel on the flame." He leaned forward, lowering his voice to a hoarse whisper. "*But there is another way.*"

The boys exchanged glances again. Rav Eliezer was known for his dramatic performances — it's what made him such a riveting teacher; but Yossi was not convinced of his sincerity.

"Rabbi Kook taught us the answer decades ago," Rabbi Eliezer went on. "'If we were destroyed, and the world was destroyed with us, by baseless hatred; we will be rebuilt, and the world will be rebuilt with us, by baseless love.'"

"But Rabbi," the boy to Gadi's right blurted out, "haven't we all already tried that? We stayed up nights, we went door to door, we spoke to the Likudnikim, we even convinced many of them to change their votes, but none of that helped in the end."

"It is still not too late, my dear students. 'God's salvation is like the blink of an eye.' What I am telling you is that you must focus your efforts on cultivating love. Love for your fellow, for God, for the Torah and the commandments. You assume that physical power is what will win this fight — that we will overwhelm them with our numbers. That's not the case. We will overwhelm them with our love. We will overwhelm them with our prayer. The people, the Torah, and the land — we are bound in an eternal bond, and if we dedicate ourselves fully to love of the first two, God will never be able to turn a deaf ear on us. He will never be able to take us away from our land. Do you understand what I am telling you?"

Yossi stared into his lap, turning these words over in his mind. The students around him nodded obediently.

"If the day does come," Rav Eliezer went on, "that we see Jewish soldiers approaching the settlements and knocking on doors, asking for our families to leave their homes..." Rav Eliezer shook his head. "They must be so overwhelmed with our love, they will be paralyzed. They will be unable to carry out their orders. Do you see what I'm saying? We need to speak to their hearts, boys. Blocking roads and burning tires is not the way." He paused, again scanning the faces of his students. "I want you to discuss among yourselves some more constructive strategies for channeling this concept into action. And I want you to come to me with your proposal, and I will help you figure out how to implement it. Do I make myself clear?"

More nodding.

"Good. You may go."

The students rose from their chairs and shuffled toward the door, but Rav Eliezer caught Yossi by the arm as he walked by.

"Yossi," he said, pulling him aside and lowering his voice. "If there's anything you need...anything at all...please, don't hesitate to ask me."

Yossi nodded, then pulled away from him, cheeks flushing in embarrassment for having been singled out.

In the months that followed, Rabbi Shlomo forbade Yossi from participating in any more political protests and insisted that he focus on his matriculation exams. Yossi sat in his dorm with his books closed in front of him, sketching pencil drawings of his home by the beach. He handed in his math and history exam booklets completely blank.

The grades would come through in August, anyway, he figured, and by then, no one would be paying any attention anymore.

NOTHING
LIKE THEM

Spring 2005

She was perched on the edge of a bar stool, resting her elbows on the bar behind her as she watched the activity in the rest of the café. Peduel didn't know for sure that it was her; he just hoped so as soon as he caught sight of her. Her hair was bleached at the tips and it tumbled down her shoulders; he had never been a fan of those hoop earrings that were all the rage, but she had a pair that somehow looked stylish rather than gaudy. She caught sight of him and gave him a knowing smile, sliding off the bar stool.

"You must be Peduel," she said.

"How did you know?" He smiled.

"You knew it was me, didn't you?"

Peduel blinked. "No, I didn't," he said.

She scrutinized him. Something about her piercing look sent a shiver down his spine.

"Yes, you did," she pronounced, and turned around to find a table.

Peduel followed her, not sure whether he felt more unnerved or intrigued. This was the first time he had allowed his friends to set him up on a blind date, and he was already wondering if it should also be the last. Ayala took a seat in the far corner of the café, facing the door.

"I always face the door," she said as Peduel sat down. "So I can see the terrorist first."

Peduel studied her face to figure out whether she was joking. The corners of her mouth were still tugged upwards in a mysterious smile.

"So what if you see him?" he challenged. "Then you'll be stuck in the corner, farthest from the exit. You won't be able to escape."

"Maybe," Ayala said, nodding to a waitress. "But also, I'll be farthest from the blast. Better chance of survival."

"Then what good does it do you to see the terrorist?"

Ayala shrugged. "I dunno. Makes me feel better."

The waitress handed them menus and Ayala began scanning hers. Peduel just watched her until she looked up. "Aren't you going to order something?"

"I already know what I want."

"You've eaten here before?"

"No. All cafés are the same."

"Oh?" She lifted an eyebrow. "And you always order the same thing?"

"Fettuccini in salsa rosa. They always have it."

"Fettuccini in salsa rosa," she repeated, narrowing her eyes again in that intense X-ray-vision look that made Peduel feel like he was under a microscope. "I don't think I've ever ordered that."

"You're missing out."

"Learn something new every day." Ayala called the waitress over. "Two fettuccini in salsa rosa," she said, "and a lemonade for me."

"Something to drink?" the waitress addressed Peduel.

"Tuborg."

"Red or green?"

"Whatever."

Ayala adjusted the asymmetrical neckline of her top, which hung teasingly off one shoulder, and Peduel wasn't sure whether it was a good thing that he was wondering what the other shoulder looked like.

"So," Peduel said. "I was told you're *datlash* as well."

Ayala nodded.

"Where did you grow up?"

"Rishon. Went to a nearby religious high school. I was caught wearing pants in tenth grade. They almost expelled me."

"How did your parents react?"

"They were mad, you know, but they got used to the idea eventually. At first I was obnoxious about it, you know, like all teenagers are, but as things settled down and my parents let me go to a secular school, I calmed down a bit." Ayala nodded at him. "You?"

Pedual looked down, raising his eyebrows briefly and letting out a little laugh. "That sounds like an awfully gentle story."

"Your parents reacted badly."

"To put it lightly."

"How old were you?"

"Sixteen. They threw me out on the street. Just like that. Refused to let me back in the house." He had told this story a million times in the past ten years, and had grown rather bored of telling it, but this time, there was something comforting about seeing Ayala wince.

"What did you do?" she asked.

"Hitchhiked to Tel Aviv. I don't know why, it just seemed like the place to go. Slept on park benches for a few months before I found the Dror organization, and they helped me get back on my feet."

"Park benches? Seriously? And your parents didn't care?"

"I don't know. I haven't been in touch with them or with any of my siblings since."

"Wow." Ayala was giving him that look again, but it was softer, kinder this time. "That's brutal."

Peduel shrugged. "You can imagine why I didn't find the religious life particularly charming."

"Suffocating." Ayala nodded. "And it sounds like your parents were very strict."

"They live in Elon Moreh. Settlers are hardcore."

"Yeah?" Ayala leaned back as the waitress set down her lemonade and popped open Peduel's beer. "I don't think I've met that many."

"Consider yourself lucky." Peduel took a swig of beer.

"There was this one kid," Ayala said, "who knocked on our door. From Gush Katif."

Peduel snorted in disgust.

"He was from one of the Bnei Akiva high schools. Yad Binyamin, I think. He told us all about his house by the sea, how he moved there when he was four, his dad is the rabbi of his settlement and an army veteran, an amputee. His politics were total nonsense, but he had a passion I couldn't help but admire. I felt kind of bad for the kid."

"He's lucky he didn't drop by *my* place. They are so full of it. I would have slammed the door in his face. I actually volunteered to participate in the disengagement, as part of my reserve duty."

"You mean, evacuating the settlers?" Ayala rested her chin on her hand. "What, like in a revenge fantasy kind of thing?"

"Of course not!" Peduel protested, blood rushing to his face. "Why would you say that? It's not about my family. They're in Samaria anyhow. It's just...I understand settlers, I know their mindset, I come from that world, and that's useful knowledge.

I'm equipped for it. I have emotional maturity they don't have. Would you stop looking at me like that?"

Ayala blinked. "Like what?"

"Like you know everything about me. It's creeping me out."

Ayala raised her eyebrows.

"What are you afraid I'm seeing, Peduel?"

"You sound like my therapist."

Ayala laughed. "I've been told I should be a therapist." Then she leaned in, and the neckline of her shirt fell away a little from her skin, making Peduel swallow. "Well," she said, "whatever it is I've seen so far, I haven't run away screaming yet, so you're probably fine." She straightened, and Peduel felt a little disappointed that the tantalizing view disappeared. Then a large bowl of pasta was lowered to further obscure it, and Peduel realized that the waitress had brought their meals.

"All right," Ayala said, rubbing her hands together. "Let's see what's so special about fettuccini with salsa rosa."

———※———

"This one's mine," Ayala said, coming to a stop in front of an apartment building and turning to face Peduel. She was hugging herself, even though the stifling Tel Aviv humidity hadn't lifted.

"Okay then," Peduel said.

They stood there, watching each other for a moment.

"Did I scare you?" Ayala asked.

"A little."

"I tend to have that effect."

Peduel detected a little sadness in her smile now. He shifted from one foot to the other.

Ayala reached out, grabbed the front of his shirt, and pulled him in, planting a solid kiss on his lips. Peduel felt a warmth surge through his body, but she pulled back before he had a chance to respond, leaning back and giving him that mysterious smile again.

"You're actually pretty cute," she said, and with that, pulled open the glass door to her building and walked inside. Peduel watched her climb up the stairs without looking back at him as the door clicked shut behind her.

As he plodded down the street toward the bus stop, he felt like he was coming out of a dream, slowly pulling together the pieces of reality and making sense of the bizarre evening he had just spent in the presence of this woman. He couldn't remember dating anyone quite that intense before. Except maybe...

Well, no, that doesn't count, he told himself firmly. *Everything was intense back then.*

What, like in a revenge fantasy kind of thing?

Ayala's remark echoed in his head, and the more distance he put between himself and her apartment, the tighter his jaw clenched. Who the hell was she to suggest that?

That night he dreamed about his therapist, the one who saw him through the Dror organization when he was still homeless and unemployed. They were sitting in her little office with the blinding white walls and the rattling old air conditioner that spewed stale, musty air. She gave him that piercing look over her cat-eye glasses, and asked:

"Why does it bother you so much that she said that?"

"You think it too, don't you?" he snapped at her in the dream.

"You think I believe that you agreed to participate in the disengagement because you want revenge on your parents?"

"Why does everyone always make the worst assumptions about me?" he yelled, jumping up from his chair.

"You are very afraid to be like them, aren't you," she said, her expression blank.

"I'm not like them at all!" he bellowed. "I'm nothing like them!" He hurled the chair at her, but it went right through her as if she were a hologram. And then she became his father as he was when Peduel saw him last: face contorted in anger, specks of spit-foam on his beard, his large knit kippa askew.

"No son of mine will violate the Sabbath willfully under this roof!" he bellowed, and Peduel was sixteen again, standing in the hallway of their home in Elon Moreh — his little sisters peeking in wide-eyed from the kitchen, still in their pink frilly dresses from the Sabbath; his mother out of sight somewhere upstairs beyond the hard stone staircase, the tiles of the hallway floor still gleaming white from the thorough scrubbing she'd given them on Friday afternoon; the scent of her handmade *burekasim* from the third Sabbath meal still hanging in the air.

"You are not my son! Get out of this house!"

Peduel woke up drenched in cold sweat, gasping for breath.

After calming his heart rate somewhat, he groped on his bedstand until his hand closed around his phone. He picked it up and flipped it open. Blinking in the glow from the screen, he tapped out a message:

Thanks for an intriguing evening. I don't think this will work out. Wish you all the best.

Lamentations

Rabbi Shlomo sat on the floor of the synagogue next to his neighbors and friends and waited for Haim Peleg to begin reading Lamentations.

Haim's voice was choked as he began:

Alas, how the city once so populous sits alone; she has become like a widow…all her friends have betrayed her and become her enemies.

His voice cracked, and he fell silent.

Rabbi Shlomo found his own eyes filling with tears, and the sniffles and sighs of grown men rose up before the Holy Ark. He rolled his body toward his prosthetic leg, using the heel as an anchor to help him push off the floor, and made his way to the *bimah*, where Haim stood hunched over in his grief. Rabbi Shlomo put a supportive arm around him, and Haim wept into his shoulder. Rabbi Shlomo wept with him for a moment; then, he gave his congregant a firm little shake in the shoulders, nodding at the book in front of him. Haim took a deep, shuddering breath, and continued reading in a faltering voice. Rabbi Shlomo stood with him, an arm on his shoulder, through the rest of the reading.

There are two major fasts in the Jewish year: a white fast, and a black fast. On Yom Kippur, the congregation was bedecked in brilliant white clothing, begging God to cleanse them of sins and purify them of iniquity; their faces tilted upward, their arms stretched wide toward the heavens. On Tisha B'Av, they were hunched over, broken; not allowed to greet one another, as they all became mourners; grieving a loss far older than any living memory, but just as sharp, just as painful in every generation as it had been for the last.

The fast of Tisha B'Av of 5765 was the blackest of the black. Rabbi Shlomo had heard a story once about the Hasidic rabbi who claimed that he didn't fast on Tisha B'Av, and who, in response to the questions from his shocked students, explained that he was so broken, so full of sorrow, on Tisha B'Av, that he couldn't dream of putting a single morsel in his mouth. Rabbi Shlomo finally understood this story as he sat listlessly on the floor of his home, his back slouched against the bookshelf. Shulamit — who always had difficulty fasting — was laid up in bed with the air conditioner on full blast, and only Yossi sat on the floor across from him. Rabbi Shlomo studied the fuzz that had grown on Yossi's face in the past week, during which, as per the custom, they were prohibited from shaving. He hadn't realized, until that moment, how much Yossi looked like a younger version of himself with his tan skin, jet black hair, and pointed features — except for his mother's wide brown eyes, which were fixed on the bay window facing the sea.

"When is midday?" Yossi asked without looking at his father.

"Soon, I expect," Rabbi Shlomo replied. As if in response, the calls of the muezzins from the neighboring villages rose up in their disharmonious wail. Yossi pushed himself to his feet and walked to the refrigerator to check the rabbinical times posted on the calendar. Then he returned to the living room and offered his father a hand. Rabbi Shlomo took it and let his son help him to his feet, and they both moved to settle on the couch. Yossi was smiling. Rabbi Shlomo scrutinized him through narrow eyes.

"Why are you so happy all of the sudden?"

"Because this is the moment where things start to turn around," Yossi said, a strange glint in his eyes. "Tisha B'Av morning is the lowest of the low. When midday comes around, we start to rise up. It's only uphill from here."

Yossi suddenly laughed, a laugh like the glimmering of sunlight off the sea in their window.

"This is where the redemption starts," he went on, breathless and wild-eyed. "We will begin to see miracles now. God will hear our prayers. There's no way He couldn't now, not after all these tears we've shed. The soldiers will come and they will be blinded by the sheer power of our pain and they won't be able to do a thing. Life will continue here as normal. I just *know* it."

Rabbi Shlomo studied his son, an odd discomfort rising within him. On the one hand, his son's words were a reflection of everything he and the rest of the anti-disengagement movement had been prophesying and preaching, and everything he wanted to believe. The Talmud teaches that even if a sharp sword rests upon one's neck, one should never desist from asking God for mercy. The youth groups had drawn up schedules of summer activities in the Gush that extended well beyond the 15th of August, and very few people had taken up the government on its offer for compensation and relocation. There seemed to be an unspoken agreement among the settler leadership that planning for the disengagement to actually happen meant admitting defeat.

On the other hand…was it really the best course of action to deny what Rabbi Shlomo had to admit was the most likely outcome? Shouldn't they at least be emotionally prepared for the possibility that the following day, the sun would set on an empty

Neve Dekalim, and that three days later, the soldiers would appear on their own doorsteps?

Rabbi Shlomo looked into his son's eyes, dazzled at the light he saw in them. Yossi had been so quiet and moody since the protest incident; it had been a long time since Rabbi Shlomo had seen him so animated, and his heart ached. The hope emanating from his son's face seemed to lift him out of the black hole of despair he had sunk into the previous night at the first note of Lamentations. He imagined extinguishing that hope, and realized that he would rather lose his other leg.

"May it be His will," he said.

WHEN TEL AVIV MET GUSH KATIF

August 19, 2005 | Ehud Hazan

Last year I dedicated a column to my misadventures in Gush Katif on the day of the human chain protest. I never dreamed I would write about it again, but somehow my editor got it into his head that the time I spent in the tiny seaside settlement of Neve Adva made me a perfect candidate to cover its evacuation. I assure you, I had no intention of being anywhere near Gush Katif during the disengagement, and when he first approached me with this harebrained idea, I flat-out refused. He spent the next several months alternating between begging, bribing, and threatening. It was the hefty bonus at the end of this month that did me in; but no less important was the free rein over content and word count. He promised not to touch a single word of this column without my approval, and that's why you are reading this sentence. I hope you're pleased with yourself, Ginzberg.

I left for Gaza in the evening. My wife hovered over me as I gathered my equipment, scowling, and when I bid her good-bye and pecked her cheek, all she had to say before stalking off toward the bedroom was, "Don't die."

An encouraging send-off.

During the drive south I tried to get into the spirit of the thing: this was finally happening. We've been holding this chunk of land for forty years without having any idea what to do with it, controlling and oppressing the local population and putting our soldiers and citizens in harm's way. I had hoped that the withdrawal would take place as part of a peace process, and I am wary of the unilateral nature of the move. I'm concerned it may undermine the authority of the Palestinian Authority. But one way or the other, it's about time we got the hell out of there. And—dammit, Ginzberg—I suppose I'm glad to witness this moment in history.

As I handed my press pass to the border policeman at Kissufim Checkpoint, I noticed a commotion on the other side of the road. After I crossed the checkpoint, I pulled over to investigate. A Palestinian woman in a cream-colored hijab was slumped on the sidewalk, sobbing and clutching her stomach. Another hijabi woman was crouched next to her, one arm around her shoulders. Nearby, an Israeli soldier was stabbing his finger at some papers in the hands of another man, who was gesturing with equal fervor. As I approached, the Israeli soldier stalked off into the security booth, and the man with the papers turned toward the women and swore heartily. He told me in Hebrew that the woman in the cream-colored hijab was due for a dangerous cancer treatment at Tel Hashomer, and that all the permits had been obtained, but the army was still giving them trouble about her papers for reasons known only to them.

I held the image of that woman's face in my mind as I continued down the dark highway, wondering whether the pullout would make it easier or harder for her to get the life-saving treatment she deserves.

My first glimpse of Neve Adva last year had been in broad daylight; nothing looked familiar under the glow of the half-moon. As I approached the gate of the town and looked out over the water, I could make out the silhouette of a dock with a small fishing boat.

The first person I encountered was Batya Karni, the head of the settlement's council. Bedecked in that horrific orange, she stood by the gate, chatting with some journalists under the weary light of a single street lamp. When I approached, she filled me in: Neve Adva was planning a peaceful evacuation. She and the other community leaders would do all they could to keep things under control.

I noticed a group of teenagers piling wood scraps and tires in a heap right behind the gate. When I inquired about them, Karni answered that the council had reached an agreement with the army to allow for some symbolic protest.

"We need to give the youth a chance to express their frustration," she explained.

I approached said frustrated youth and caught the eye of a swarthy kid with a large knit kippa and *tzitzit* strings swinging haphazardly at his waist. He looked vaguely familiar, but he narrowed his eyes in suspicion when I asked him for his name. He demanded to know who I was and what paper I write for first. When I told him, he spat on the ground in front of me and turned his back.

Another group of teens sat in a circle with a guitar. I settled on the ground nearby to watch their vigil: melancholy singing interspersed with melodramatic little speeches and what seemed like quotes from various rabbis I'd never heard of.

"But seriously, why are you here?" came a cutting voice, and I turned to face the teen who had spat at me earlier, twisting around to glower at me from the circle. He gestured sharply past my shoulder. "Why don't you go interview your friends in that village instead of drawing antisemitic caricatures of settlers?"

It took a great deal of effort to refrain from rolling my eyes.

"Don't, Yossi." The one sitting next to him, another orange-clad young man with long sidecurls, nudged his arm. "You're only making it worse."

"How could I make it any worse?" Yossi retorted. "He writes for the Israeli *Der Stürmer*. He took advantage of my father's kindness last year when his car broke down, and now he's back here to spit in our faces."

Ah. So that's why he looked familiar.

"He and his buddies up in Tel Aviv are the ones who brainwashed Sharon into destroying our homes," he was saying.

"Maybe if you were nicer to me, I would be more inclined to portray you sympathetically," I suggested.

"Maybe if we were nicer to the Nazis, they wouldn't have murdered six million of us," he shot back before turning away.

I glanced at my watch: it had taken approximately fourteen minutes, forty-seven seconds from the moment I left my car until I got called a Nazi.

I did manage to chat with some slightly less belligerent teens. I learned that most of them weren't even from Neve Adva: they were youth from religious Zionist communities all over, especially the more radical pockets of Samaria. I wondered how they had slipped in to the Strip, given how tight security had been at Kissufim Checkpoint, but they refused to tell me. What they were eager to share was their goal: to make the IDF's job as difficult as possible.

"Those soldiers will see that the entire nation of Israel is here, supporting the settlement," gushed one young woman from Kiryat Arba. "They won't be able to look these families in the eye and make them leave their homes."

When I asked why she thought this tactic hadn't worked in the settlements that had been evacuated in the preceding days, she simply glared at me.

It was long past midnight when the conversations petered out. I set up camp on the beachfront near the dock and lay down, marveling at the luminous sky. It's easy to forget how many stars are up there behind the smog and light pollution of Tel Aviv. I fell asleep to the lull of the waves.

Next I knew, the sun was bright. I washed my face in the surf and headed back toward the settlement's gate, where the teens from last night were handing out fresh rolls and bags of chocolate milk. Batya Karni was still standing by the security booth next to the gate, and she had a wild-eyed, overtired look about her.

The first troops appeared on the horizon at around 8:00 AM, marching alongside a bulldozer. Several buses pulled up behind them. The teenagers lit their pyre behind the gate, and the stench of burning rubber filled the air. It didn't take long for the soldiers to put out the flames. They began sawing the settlement's gate off its hinges. Then the bulldozer took over, pushing in the gate and clearing away the pile of burnt rubble. One row of soldiers formed a ring around the settlement, while the others — maybe 100 or so — lined up in silent rows behind the gate. They wore hydration packs and navy baseball caps with IDF insignia. I approached them, but they just shook their heads and stared ahead. The teenagers at the barbed wire fence bombarded them with insults: "Robots! Nazis! Criminals!" Batya Karni ushered the kids away after a few minutes. In the quiet that followed, I spotted a few soldiers shuffling their feet.

With the entrance cleared, the soldiers began entering the settlement. Groups of twenty or thirty soldiers established themselves as an intimidating human fence around each house, while a smaller team of three or four soldiers knocked on the front door.

I followed one unit to the Asaf household. The commander knocked on the door and called the names of the family members, who predictably refused to open it. The commander called through the door that he would be back in thirty minutes, and if they did not open the door then, the soldiers would be forced to break in.

This disengagement thing seemed to involve a lot more standing around than I had seen in the news.

I decided to move ahead of them to the rabbi's house. After all, as his crazy son had reminded me, he did me a kindness last year, and I wanted to check in on him. No one answered when I knocked on the door.

"Rabbi Shlomo?" I called. "It's Ehud Hazan, the journalist. The army isn't here yet."

The handle turned and the door pulled open a crack. Shulamit, Rabbi Shlomo's wife, peered out at me. Her eyes were red and dark with exhaustion.

"Good morning," I said. "May I come in?"

"Shlomo is at the synagogue," she said. "And if you don't mind, I'd rather you didn't." She shut the door before I could say another word.

So I headed for the synagogue, and found it barricaded. The group of teens I had spoken with the previous night was setting up barbed wire around the perimeter of the roof. I could hear the guitar playing up there, and it sounded like they were singing and dancing and clapping. The army seemed to be ignoring them for the time being. I abandoned my search for Rabbi Shlomo and returned to the Asaf household, where the soldiers were still waiting outside, staring at the ground.

One by one, the families emerged from their homes. Most of them walked out to their cars or to the buses waiting for them outside the gates. There were a few cases where there was resistance. A man was dragged from his doorstep by four soldiers, one for each limb. He was shouting something about Sharon's corrupt government and President Bush. A woman who appeared to be his wife followed, weeping; a clump of small children clung to her floor-length skirt. A female soldier carried another child behind them, and beneath the sunglasses I could see a red puffiness around her eyes.

As the evacuation of the families from their homes concluded, the soldiers approached the synagogue. I had seen the scenes from Neve Dekalim and Kfar Darom, and I was anticipating a similar clash, given the foaming-at-the-mouth furor I had witnessed the previous night, but there were no buckets of acid or rocks thrown. The soldiers were lifted to the rooftop in a shipping container suspended from a crane. They cut the wires and infiltrated the little fortress the teens had built, and proceeded to carry the teens from the rooftop. There was a lot of resistance and kicking and screaming, but the deed was done with calm conviction. The soldiers carried out their orders, as the slogan went, with determination and sensitivity. The soldier-settler tangles were lowered to the ground in batches, where they shuffled toward the gates. The soldiers then passed the teens to other soldiers who were waiting there to drag them onto the buses.

I spotted a little girl I recognized—the older sister of that toddler-barnacle I'd been photographed with during my last trip to Neve Adva—dropping to her knees in front of her home with a potted plant and a water bottle in her arms. As I watched, she set it down and dug a hole in the dirt with her hands, crying and singing to herself. Then she removed the plant from its pot and rested it in the hole, packing dirt around it. A female soldier stood behind her as she did this, her jaw set as though trying not to cry, and waited until the girl had watered the plant before taking her hand and leading her back into the house—where I presume her mother was still packing up.

I must be honest with you. That I supported the evacuation wholeheartedly is no secret. You'd think I would feel satisfied, watching the IDF carry out an operation I approve of for a change. That's how I had felt glancing at the headlines in the news. Yet watching the events unfold before my own eyes, it was hard not to be moved by the raw pain before me.

It was then that the irony of the situation really struck me. Here I was, a staunch left-winger who believes sincerely in the rights of Palestinians to this land, and feels sympathy for the suffering they endured when they were forced to leave their homes in 1948 and live under foreign occupation for the past forty years; and here, for the last six months or so, I'd been relating to the settlers—like much of the media—with some combination of mockery and contempt. I believed they were so obsessed with retaining every grain of sand in their vision of Greater Israel that they were blind to what it cost us as a people; willing to do anything, including acts of violence, to hold on to what the Israeli government had decided they must lose, and to avoid being uprooted from their homes and forced to leave everything they cherished behind.

The parallel had never occurred to me before.

Why did I have to be standing in the impossible heat of a late August day, watching tears make their way down the faces of soldiers and settlers alike, to feel that same sympathy for *them?*

But I'll tell you what really succeeded in piercing my cold, dead, cynical heart. Promise you won't laugh.

It was when I saw the rabbi emerging from the synagogue doors, holding a Torah scroll.

Stay with me.

It was a Sephardic-style scroll, encased in a decorative silver-plated chest, its handles peeking out of the top and crowned with silver pomegranates. It looked exactly like the one in the photos my father had shown me of my grandfather, a rabbi from Baghdad, carrying the community's Torah scroll onto the tarmac at Ben Gurion Airport.

My grandfather did not like to speak of his life in Iraq, and he died when I was still a boy. The community he came from was never mentioned in history class. These days the history of Jews in Islamic lands is an elective unit on the matriculation exams; when I was in high school, it wasn't even on the curriculum. When I was in college, I learned that Jews had lived in Iraq for 2,600 years, and that my grandfather and the rest of his community were expelled by the Iraqi government under threat of Nazi-style concentration camps in 1951. My father tells me that the family had been quite wealthy, but all their assets were seized by the Iraqi government before they were expelled. The terrible pogrom of 1941, the Farhud, had claimed the lives of my great-grandparents, my grandmother, two of my aunts, and several cousins.

The expression on Rabbi Shlomo's face — a mix of devastation, confusion, determination, and hope — was eerily similar to the expression on the face of my grandfather in that photo.

That, dear readers, is when my momentary lapse in sanity occurred.

I, Ehud Hazan, sworn atheist, Meretz voter, Tel Avivi, columnist for several left-wing publications, and all-around jackass, covered my head with my hand, approached the rabbi and the scroll, and kissed it like a goddamn *mizrochnik*.

I neither confirm nor deny the descent of a tear down my cheek as I did this.

The rabbi — in an impressive feat of upper body strength — shifted the weight of the scroll to one arm, reached out, and gave me a firm pat on the shoulder. I retreated to the wall of the synagogue to try to recover my dignity. When I looked up, I caught a glimpse of his prayer shawl disappearing up the steps to one of the buses.

Don't be alarmed, my faithful readers. I'm still an atheist, I still plan to vote Meretz, I still love to hate my sardine can on Tchernikovsky, my editor has miraculously not fired me yet (though we still haven't run this column, so no guarantees), and I'm definitely still a jackass. I must admit, however, that I will never look at settlers quite the same way.

When I got home that night, my wife had a cold beer waiting for me, and she waited until I had downed the entire thing before saying a word. "So," she said. "You didn't die."

But something in me did, dear readers. Something in me did.

COMMENTARY ON THE FORMER PROPHETS

*There are three graces: the grace of a wife
to her husband, the grace of a hometown
to its inhabitants, and the grace of an
acquired item to its purchaser.*

Rabbi Shlomo couldn't get that line out of his head as he and his wife watched the sun set over the sea from the bay window of their home on August 17th, 2005.

It was true, what they said about one's life flashing before one's eyes before death; he knew, because that's what happened when his leg was blown off by a mortar shell and he lay there bleeding out on the battlefield. There was a stillness, a ringing silence, and scenes from his childhood played before his eyes, the sound of his mother singing a lullaby, before waking suddenly to intense, all-consuming pain at Rambam Hospital in Haifa.

And now, despite himself, the images of the past eleven years in Neve Adva were flashing through his mind. That first moment on the beach, understanding that this was going to be his home. His daughters twirling about in the sand, laughing and chasing each other. That first Shabbat in the suffocating heat without air conditioning, when he'd slept under the stars. The wedding he'd officiated for Aharon Cohen. The funeral he'd officiated for Aharon Cohen. The flushed pink cheeks of his eldest daughter as she shared the news that she and her boyfriend had gotten engaged. The moment that same daughter stepped into their home with her firstborn wrapped tightly in a blanket.

Shulamit shifted in her armchair, sighing deeply, and her voice jerked Shlomo out of his reverie.

"It's too quiet," she said.

Rabbi Shlomo reached out to clasp her hand.

"Yossi is out with his friends," he said. "By the gate. I think they're planning to stay there all night. I guess no one intends to get any sleep."

"Who can sleep?"

"You should." Rabbi Shlomo stood from his armchair, wincing as usual when he shifted his weight onto his prosthetic leg. He leaned down to kiss her forehead. "You need your sleep."

"And you don't?"

"I need to be in the synagogue."

"You mean, the community needs you to be in the synagogue."

"No," Shlomo said, staring across the room at the door. "I'm the captain of the ship and the synagogue is my bridge. I need to be there."

"Because the ship is going down?"

Rabbi Shlomo did not answer. He strode to the bookcase to gather his prayer book and tucked the velvet pouch that held his prayer shawl and *tefillin* under his arm.

"One last walk through the house?" Shulamit stood and took him by the elbow.

"One last walk."

They walked silently side by side, slowly moving from one room to the next, and Rabbi Shlomo tried to etch every corner, every crack into his memory. Goodbye to the kitchen, with its cheerful marble countertops, and the aroma of chicken soup and fresh-baked challah every Friday night; goodbye to the living room, with the plump armchairs facing the sea, where he'd spent long Shabbat afternoons playing chess with his daughters and studying *Mesillat Yesharim* with Yossi; goodbye to the bedrooms, with the wooden bedframes and four-doored wardrobes covered in stickers and handmade birthday cards for his teenagers; goodbye to the room he shared with his wife for ten years, with its purple curtains, now faded to a dull lavender from the rays of harsh sunlight they had softened on their way into the room. Shulamit's face dripped with silent tears, but Rabbi Shlomo could feel nothing. It was like a horrible dream, and somehow, Rabbi Shlomo still held out hope that he would wake.

Finally, they made their way to the door and held each other in a long, clinging embrace.

"Sleep well," Rabbi Shlomo whispered, then kissed his wife on the lips. He opened the door, and his hand instinctively shot to the painted glass mezuzah case hanging on the doorframe. He turned his head to look at it and lingered for a moment, gazing without seeing, and then jerked his hand away and kissed his fingers, shuffling down the steps and out into the dusk.

Rabbi Shlomo swung the synagogue door open and scanned the sanctuary. A few men were scattered throughout the rows of wooden benches circling the *bimah*, the raised wooden platform at the center of the room. Ahead of the *bimah* — toward Jerusalem in the northeast — was the Holy Ark, the cabinet that contained the settlement's one precious Torah scroll. A velvet curtain hung over the doors, with appliquéd letters in brilliantly painted silk that read: "A tree of life is she for those who cling to her," and below that, "In memory of Aharon ben Tzvi HaCohen, HY"D."

The visiting youth eventually shuffled into the synagogue and Rabbi Shlomo led them in the evening prayers. He was too distracted to focus, however. He scanned them, looking for Yossi, but couldn't find him. They stayed and sang for a while. Normally Rabbi Shlomo would join them, letting the melodies of yearning and the words of supplication penetrate, but he didn't this time, instead pacing near the wide windows of the building, thinking about how permeable it was, how unprotected.

During the worst days of the Second Intifada there had been a discussion in the council about installing bars over the windows after a terrorist broke into a public building in a nearby settlement and killed two teenagers with an ax. Of course, like with most projects, they never found the funds for it, and eventually the idea fell by the wayside as the horror of that murder faded and people returned to their normal routines. Most of the time he was grateful; looking at the sea through those bars would have felt like a betrayal of the reason he'd come here to begin with. Today, he wished the project had been completed. Just to give them some more time.

When the teens dispersed, a handful of men remained in the prayer hall, paired off, and began murmuring over their *Gemaras*. Rabbi Shlomo had been studying Tractate Yoma recently, but he felt little desire to pick it up as usual. So he paused by the bookshelves near the door, scanning the tattered spines, and his gaze rested on a volume toward the bottom. Its spine was made of some brown leather-like material, so worn with age that the strings from the binding were exposed. It reminded him of the books on the shelf of the Caro synagogue in Safed. Incredibly old, and out of place on the synagogue bookshelf. He swung the hip of his good leg to the floor, sitting down to get a better look, and carefully slid the book off the shelf. There was no lettering on the cover. It felt strangely heavy. He turned it over in his hands, examining the crackled brown cover, and then opened it. A sprinkle of brown flakes fell to the floor. On the title page was an elaborate drawing of pillars and a canopy, framing the words: *Commentary on the Former Prophets*, by Don Isaac Abarbanel.

Rabbi Shlomo squinted down at it through his glasses. He'd studied for ten years at Har Etzion Yeshiva, through the hesder program and rabbinical school, but somehow he could not recall reading Abarbanel on the Former Prophets. And this book seemed unfathomably old. He searched for the Hebrew publication date. *Tav, mem, vav* ... 5446. He did a quick calculation in his head and his eyes widened. 1686. What was a 300-year-old book doing here?!

Rabbi Shlomo reached up to place the book on a higher shelf and rolled toward his missing leg, using the inert plastic of the prosthesis as a lever to begin his laborious ascent from the floor. It was a movement he'd gotten so used to now, after twenty-three years, that it came as second nature; but in the first year after the injury, getting onto the floor and up again felt like an impossible task. He'd had two little daughters at home at the time, and watching the ease with which Shulamit knelt and squatted to pick them up or play with them had sometimes made his eyes mist in frustration.

Forget living on the front lines with their support and encouragement and gratitude, he thought bitterly as he scooped up the old book and carried it to his usual spot by the *bimah. I literally gave my right leg for this country, and this is how they repay me?*

He sat down and placed the book carefully on the lectern in front of him. The pages were thick and browned with age, but the ink was deep black, making the words jump out at him. There was a disorienting mess of pages with Latin letters, but he carefully turned the pages until he reached the foreword for the book of Joshua.

I am the man Isaac... it read. *I was content in my home, a home and an inherited fortune, a home full of the blessings of God in the illustrious Lisbon, a city and a mother in the kingdom of Portugal...*

Rabbi Shlomo stared at the page in front of him.

Don Isaac Abarbanel. The great Sephardic statesman and scholar. The man who personally pleaded with the cruel Catholic Monarchs to reverse their evil decree. The man who was expelled from Spain with his people in 1492.

Rabbi Shlomo leaned forward eagerly, drinking in Abarbanel's words. In the preface to the book of Joshua, Abarbanel described the story of his conflict with the new king of Portugal and his flight to Castile in great detail.

"...And he took everything I had, my land and my belongings, leaving me with not a remnant.... I cried out, 'Redeem me, O King, is it good for you to steal? Will the judge of all the land not do justice?'"

Rabbi Shlomo pictured King João II as an enormous man with Ariel Sharon's white hair, sagging chin, and full-bellied chortle.

"Why did my God not hear me even though I cried out and implored Him?" lamented Abarbanel, and Rabbi Shlomo felt tears pricking at his eyes.

He read and read, skimming through the commentaries but thirstily drinking in every word of the prefaces, where Abarbanel described his personal trials and travails. He was so absorbed that he didn't notice the other men leaving, one by one, even when they bid him goodbye and clapped him on the shoulder. Long into the night, he plowed his way through the commentaries on the book of Joshua, and the book of Judges, and both Samuels, until his eyelids drooped and his vision swam with Hebrew letters...and then he reached the preface to Kings I, and Abarbanel's description of the expulsion from Spain.

I spoke to the king three times, I begged him, saying, "Redeem us,

O King! Why do you do this to your servants?" ...I called upon those who were fond of me, who were seeing the king, to beg for my people, and nobles came together to speak to the king with all their power to recall the decree...and like a deaf cobra that closes its ear, he would not respond to any of them; and the queen stands by his right side.... We toiled and never rested, and I was not tranquil or silent and I did not rest....

"Rabbi Shlomo Toledano?"

Rabbi Shlomo started. He hadn't noticed when the synagogue fell silent hours before or when the singing and talking from outside faded, but the sound of the voice jerked him out of his trance. He looked up. Standing in front of him was an old man with a huge white beard, dressed rather strangely, in what looked somewhat like traditional Moroccan robes, but his skin was pale. He had fierce, sparkling brown eyes. Rabbi Shlomo squinted up at him, trying to remember if he had ever seen this man before. He could not recall.

"May I?" the man said, pulling up a folding chair and seating himself in front of Rabbi Shlomo.

"Of...of course," Rabbi Shlomo stuttered. "Of course. Who...with whom do I have the honor?"

"Yitzchak," said the man. He had an odd accent that Rabbi Shlomo couldn't quite place, but it certainly didn't sound Moroccan.

"Have we...met before?"

"Not exactly." The man nodded at the book. "What are you learning?"

"Abarbanel on the Former Prophets."

"Abravanel," said the man.

Rabbi Shlomo blinked. "Excuse me?"

"It's pronounced Abravanel." He offered no further explanation as he carefully slid the book from beneath Rabbi Shlomo's hands and examined it. "Remarkable," he muttered.

"Yes...that is why I didn't notice you come in," Rabbi Shlomo said. "I'm floored by the parallels between our time and what he describes."

"Oh?" Yitzchak raised an eyebrow at him.

"Of course," Rabbi Shlomo said, reaching for the book. Yitzchak reluctantly handed it to him. "Listen to this: 'And the people heard the evil decree and they mourned, and in every place where the king's orders and his edict reached, there was great mourning for the Jews...as there had not been since the day of the expulsion of Judah from his land to a foreign land...and they went, with no strength, three hundred thousand people and I among them, from youth to old man, children and women, in one day, from all the provinces of the king, to wherever the wind blew...'"

"You compare those scenes to the disengagement from Gaza?"

"Well, of course," Rabbi Shlomo said, his eyebrows furrowing slightly.

Yitzchak made a scoffing noise. "Surely you jest."

Rabbi Shlomo set his jaw, recoiling somewhat from the man.

"The Jews of *Sepharad*," Yitzchak continued, "were sent out of a land not their own, with no money, no belongings, and no future. You leave with all the possessions you desire; you will be resettled in the land of your forefathers! If only the Sephardim were a fraction so fortunate!" He cast a look around the synagogue. "Was this place not the land of the Philistines?"

Rabbi Shlomo gave him a hard look. "I don't know who you are or where you came from," he said sharply, "or what business you have here, but you have some nerve coming here to tell me that this expulsion is anything less than a disastrous betrayal and a catastrophe for the Jewish people. Jews have lived in Gaza since the days of the Maccabees. This land was given to us by the Holy One in a war of defense. And it holds the same status as our true fatherland — Judea and Samaria, whose every hilltop and valley is mentioned by the Prophets. What happens here sets a precedent for what happens there. This *is* a part of the land promised to us by God. By giving it up we are spitting in His face."

Yitzchak looked deep into Rabbi Shlomo's eyes, and Rabbi Shlomo felt a tingle go down his spine.

"Do you know," Yitzchak said quietly, "what the queen of Castilla — Isabel, *yimach shema* — " he spat on the ground — "do you know what she said to Abravanel when he went to her to plead his case?"

Rabbi Shlomo failed to see what this had to do with the topic at hand, but something about the intense fire in Yitzchak's eyes made him forget his tongue.

"The Lord opened the mouth of the she-donkey," Yitzchak went on. "She said: 'Do you believe that this comes upon you from us? The Lord hath put this thing into the heart of the king.'"

Rabbi Shlomo finally tore his eyes away from Yitzchak's and cast them to the ground. He tried to swallow the lump in his throat.

"You are saying this is God's decree?" he asked in a thin voice.

"All is God's decree," Yitzchak nodded, "is it not?"

"But *why*?" Rabbi Shlomo blurted, and finally daring to ask the question, he could not stop the torrent: "*Why*? Why would God do this to us?! All the members of my community are righteous people! The people of Gush Katif are the salt of the earth, the bedrock of the nation of Israel! How could He do this? How could He let our government — a Jewish government — how could He let them betray us like this?" He paused. "How could *He* betray us like this?"

Yitzchak was nodding. "Yes…yes," he said softly. "I know what you mean."

They sat silently for a few moments, and Rabbi Shlomo's face reddened a little, ashamed at his outburst.

"But with all due respect," Yitzchak went on, "I believe *why* is the wrong question to be asking now."

Rabbi Shlomo waited, watching the strange man intently.

"Wondrous are the ways of God. Only He can know why. The right question is, 'What now?'"

"What now?" Rabbi Shlomo echoed.

"Asking why will only make you angry," Yitzchak went on. "In every generation, there were a thousand reasons to ask why. And in every generation, we asked instead: what now? How do we rebuild what we've lost? How do we find meaning in our suffering? How do we leave a better world for our children? How do we give our people hope? How do we bring ourselves closer to redemption?" Yitzchak reached out and clutched Rabbi Shlomo's shoulder, his eyes aflame. "Oh, Rabbi Shlomo, it's so close. *So close.*"

"That's what we always say," Rabbi Shlomo muttered. "That's what Abarbanel — Abravanel — said." He tapped the book on the stand in front of him. "After the expulsion he insisted that the redemption was imminent, didn't he? He even calculated it, which we are not supposed to do, saying that it would happen mere years after the expulsion from Spain. And here we are, five hundred years later..."

"Yes!" Yitzchak's voice was breathless. "Here we are! Look around you! Just look, Rabbi Shlomo! Jewish sovereignty in the Holy Land for the first time since the days of the Hasmoneans! Unimaginable wealth — even the poorest Jews are richer than the average Jew from Abravanel's time! The prophecies of the Latter Prophets fulfilled, down to the word — vineyards in the hills of Judea, the voices of song and laughter — in the Holy Tongue! — echoing in the streets of Jerusalem! Who could have dreamed it? I could not have dreamed it!"

"Well...well, of course," Rabbi Shlomo said, "but —"

"'Of course'?! How can you say 'of course'?!" Yitzchak laughed and called up to the ceiling, slapping a hand on his knee: "I tell him that the words of Isaiah have come to pass before his very eyes, and he says 'of course'!"

"And yet, the full redemption has not come," Rabbi Shlomo said, "and for the first time in history, Jews are expelling other Jews from the Holy Land…"

"Listen to me, Rabbi Shlomo Toledano," said Yitzchak, grabbing Rabbi Shlomo by the shoulders and gazing deep into his eyes. "This is but one chapter in a very long story that *will* have a happy ending. You are closer to that ending than I ever was — and see how impatient you are. I was impatient too, and yes, I miscalculated, and I was wrong about a great many things. But I was not wrong about this. I gave my people hope. You must have hope," he rasped, "and you must give your people hope."

Before Rabbi Shlomo could register what he could possibly have meant by that, there was a loud bang on the door. Rabbi Shlomo started and twisted away, freeing himself from Yitzchak's grip. Someone was rattling the handles. Rabbi Shlomo took a deep breath and turned around to respond to Yitzchak — but he was gone.

All that was in front of him was an empty chair.

Rabbi Shlomo blinked, searching the room, but the man was nowhere to be seen.

"Is someone in there?" called a voice from outside the door.

Rabbi Shlomo rubbed his eyes vigorously. He felt woozy and disoriented. Had he been asleep? Had it been a dream?

He looked down at the ancient book still open in front of him, mulling over the last few things the man had said, and a thought suddenly hit him: *Portuguese.*

The man's accent was Portuguese.

Rabbi Shlomo stared at the book, unseeing, for a few more moments. Then he closed it very gently and stood up, wincing as he shifted his weight onto his bad leg. He raised the book to his lips and kissed it.

He peered through the windows. Soldiers were setting up ladders now, and a crane was rolling toward the building with a giant shipping container dangling from its hook. The IDF seemed to be ignoring him for the moment, in favor of getting the teenagers off the rooftop. He hadn't even heard them go up there, or their chanting, dancing, or singing.

He donned his prayer shawl and his *tefillin* and began to pray, tuning out the commotion from above and around him. *"Hasten and bring blessing and peace from the four corners of the earth,"* he murmured, clutching his *tzitzit* fringes to his heart, *"and break the yoke of the gentiles from upon our necks, and have us soon walking upright to our land…"*

He finished his prayers as the tumult outside died down. He kissed his prayer book and slid it into his velvet prayer shawl case. Then he tore down one of the curtains hanging from the windows, and carefully wrapped Abravanel's book in the cloth. This he tucked safely into the case next to the prayer book.

Then he approached the Ark. He drew back the curtain, and stroked the embossed silver coat of the Sephardic Torah case that housed the scroll. Tears rolling down his cheeks, he hoisted the case out of the Ark and ascended the *bimah*, singing softly as the drilling and hammering began to sound from the entrance. There he stood, holding his Torah, waiting for the Jewish soldiers of the Land of Zion and Jerusalem to burst through the doors.

ICED TEA

Tali started awake with a yelp, clutching at the stiff army-issue sheet that covered her. She sat bolt upright in bed, clutching her chest and trying to slow her breath.

A dream. It was only a dream.

She squinted at the window; there was a faint blue staining the black outside, and she sighed. Her alarm would probably be going off soon anyway. No use trying to get back to sleep.

She dressed quietly to avoid waking her bunkmates, and headed for the showers, hoping there would still be hot water left over from last night. It was August, and they were stationed out in the godforsaken desert; chances were good.

She washed her hair aggressively, as though trying to rid her head of the disturbing images it had played for her in her sleep. She'd been expecting some anxiety dreams about the evacuations; she'd seen some rough scenes over the past few days, and she herself had warned her soldiers about the possible effects. Nonetheless, the dream last night managed to rattle her: in the dream, she'd broken into a house only to discover her father there, shouting and spewing sunflower seed shells every which way.

It made no sense, of course, given that her father was the strongest supporter of the disengagement in the family. But she hated when he yelled at her.

The mess hall was quiet that morning; a few murmurs were audible over the clink of the silverware. The smells of cooked egg and oily *burekasim* made Tali gag. She loaded her plate with slices of bread spread with white farmer's cheese and added some bell peppers and cucumbers to eat with them, but it took her a while to coax these things into her mouth, even after her coffee. One of her colleagues saw her scowling at her breakfast and asked if he could get her something, and she just glared at him.

On her way out to the army transport, she spotted one of the orange ribbons that had been tied to the fence by teenagers from the nearby settlements a few weeks before. It had been ripped off the fence and trampled on, and now lay caught in the thorns of a bramble by the gate. She picked it up, fingering it, then folded it gently and dropped it into a nearby trash can.

Neve Adva shimmered in the heat as Tali's unit marched in a solid line toward its gates. The air was so thick, Tali felt as though she were breathing in the ocean, and there was no merciful sea breeze to lighten its weight. She swallowed hard, squinting in the harsh sunlight reflecting off the sand, trying to make sense of the mirage-like shapes up ahead. The blob of green was the gate, but there was probably a barricade behind it — tires and who knows what else that the hilltop youth planned to burn.

She'd been training for this mission for months, and as she led her soldiers, their footsteps muffled by the soft sand, she tried to go over the data in her mind. They'd been given files on each of the families, with pictures and basic facts about each family member they would be evacuating from their homes. There were 23 families in the settlement altogether. Tali was the commander of the unit that would be evacuating four houses facing the beach front. The Cohens, the Skolniks, the Steinmans, and the Pelegs. Cohens: a widow, Talia, 32, with four children, aged 2, 4, 6, and 8. Husband, Aharon, killed by a mortar shell near the fence of the settlement two years ago. Skolniks: Moshe, 46; Bruria, 43; two sons, both serving in the army, not expected to be home; Moshe's elderly father, Itzik, 76. Holocaust survivor, the file had said, and she had winced when she read it. She was expecting to be called a Nazi by the settlers — they'd practiced it a lot during drills — but being called a Nazi by someone who had faced the actual Nazis was something else entirely.

Steinman: Tuvia, 34; Moriah, 30; three children, aged 2, 4, and 5, and the file said another was expected in October. That would make her ... Tali had counted down ... seven months pregnant.

They had practiced proper evacuation technique: breaking human chains, dragging thrashing adults out of buildings, one soldier for each limb. The young women in her unit really got into the spirit of the thing. Keren had stuffed her shirt with a blanket, tied her hair with a scarf, and cried out "Oh! Oh! I'm giving birth!" as Tali and three others carried her to the other side of the room. Rotem had sniggered and lost her grip. Tali made her clean the bathrooms for a week as a penalty.

Pelegs: Tova, 43; Haim, 46; five children, aged 15, 13, 11, 9, and 6.

And then, of course, there would be the infiltrators. Fanatic youth from around the country who had come to fortify the settlements, to help the settlers, and to put more bodies in the path of the bulldozers. They'd been the main source of violence in the settlements that had already been evacuated, barricading themselves on rooftops, burning tires, pouring caustic materials on soldiers. Tali — whose unit had been in the outer circles of defense in the days before and had not come in direct contact with the settlers — had been briefed on the events of the previous few days, and it was not just the impossible heat that was making her sweat as she drew closer to Neve Adva.

The shapes became sharper as she closed the distance. She could see several cameramen crowding around the gate, and soldiers working the saws. Good, they were already breaking through the barricade. A bulldozer stood at the ready, the driver wiping his brow. And beyond the rising steam from the ashes of the barricade, figures of young men, pacing, like the lions at the Ramat Gan Safari.

She halted her unit several meters in front of the gate and turned around to remind her soldiers to drink. She choked on the acrid smoke still floating on the air from the burned tires and it took several coughing fits before she was able to get the words out. She searched the faces of her soldiers, beneath the bills of their navy-blue baseball caps. She knew how weary they were; none of them could have slept very well last night. But the sunglasses hid the bags under their eyes and they looked stoic enough.

The lineup reminded her of her trip to Masada with the Scouts. An awkward, gangly seventh-grader, Tali had never enjoyed hiking, but she hadn't dared to mention this to anyone. All it took was her father's cold look when she expressed any ambivalence about joining Scouts in the first place to know that there would be no getting out of it. The counselor would line them up like this and play stupid drinking games with them — drinking water, that is — and the game she played with herself was to see how often she could get away with *not* doing whatever the counselor told her without anyone noticing. She wasn't particularly popular, either, and it took a while for the group to realize that she wasn't among them. She was found unconscious, dehydrated and well on her way to heatstroke, by another group on Masada. She was already halfway to Soroka Hospital in an ambulance before the counselor was notified.

She remembered her father's clenched jaw, crossed arms, and furrowed brow far more clearly than her mother's embrace and sympathetic words when they came to see her at the hospital.

"Everybody drink," she repeated. "Not a single one of you had better faint on me."

Her father wore that same disapproving scowl when she hadn't been accepted into any elite units in the army like her brothers had. Having a "jobnik" daughter had never quite squared with his visions of the future, it seemed. When she was offered the opportunity to take the commanders' course, she jumped on it, even though she didn't particularly care for the army. A little prestige, she'd figured, to soften that scowl, and a little extra time in the army to regroup and figure out a career path that wouldn't deepen it. She'd hidden her art projects in shoeboxes under her bed, and when she had expressed an interest in the art program at her high school, her mother was enthusiastic; but as soon as her dad found out about it, the party was over. Her mother never stood up to him on things like this. Biology major it was.

It was only when Tali informed him that she'd be commanding an evacuation unit that the scowl had turned into a smile. "Well!" he'd said, clapping her on the shoulder. "Your army career isn't turning out to be completely useless after all." He lived closer to the base than her mother did, and Tali found herself spending more and more time with him after joining the army. They watched the protests on television together. Her father would rant at the screen in a sort of frenzy of moral rage, seething and spitting out sunflower seed shells. "Those self-righteous ingrates," he'd spit. "Can't even see what they are leeching from our country, don't even care how many soldiers have died to protect their precious sandboxes. They can take their orange ribbons and hang themselves."

Tali would watch with him, and for a change, she had to agree. According to these settlers, merely by force of following orders, she would be a willing partner in an atrocity against the Jewish people, to use their terminology, no less grievous than the Holocaust or the expulsion from Spain.

Her own grandparents were kicked out of Tunisia. No one sent buses to bring *them* to a four-star hotel, courtesy of the state, while waiting to be resettled. They bribed and begged their way to Israel, getting cheated, robbed, and raped along the way, and no one handed them a new house when they got there.

"Hey, Lieutenant!"

The voice jerked her from her reverie, and she turned sharply toward the gate. The way had been cleared, and the teenagers had disappeared; instead, a man with wavy gray hair, a loose T-shirt, and jeans was walking toward her. Tali thought he might be a journalist, and she wasn't supposed to talk to those without permission — although he wasn't carrying a camera or notebook. Most striking, though, was his expression: in sharp contrast to the grim faces surrounding Tali, his eyes twinkled, as though enjoying a private joke. She searched his face, wondering what was so funny.

"Press," he said, whipping a press pass from his pocket. Tali glared at it. "I was wondering if you wouldn't mind — "

"Hazan!" Tali stood up straighter at the bark of her commanding officer, though his voice sounded warmer than usual. Captain Gabbai sauntered over and clapped the man on the back. "Long time no see, eh? What the hell are you doing here?"

"Don't even ask," said the reporter.

"You harassing my troops again?"

"I was hoping the young lady here — "

"Tough luck, *neshama*, none of them are authorized to talk to you, you might as well interview the telephone pole. Cahana!"

Tali snapped to attention.

"Move out to your charges," Captain Gabbai ordered. "The kids are probably barricading themselves in the synagogue. We'll get to them last."

Tali nodded, turned away from the captain — who was cordially steering his journalist friend out of the way — and gave the order to march. She took a deep breath and led her troops into the settlement.

———※———

The first home along the beach was the Cohens'. It was a big house, almost like the ones the millionaires had in Tali's native Herzliya, with sand-stained white stucco, a tiled red roof and several balconies. Tali waited until her soldiers were in position, surrounding the house, before walking up the steps and the garden path to the front door.

She hesitated, absently teasing curls out from the clip at the back of her head. Images flashed through her mind: the footage from Neve Dekalim she had seen on television the other night. Settlers screaming and throwing things, soldiers being wheeled into ambulances. Settlers chanting, "Jews don't expel Jews! Jews don't expel Jews!" A woman holding up a child, screeching at the soldiers, "Look into his eyes! You will have nightmares about these eyes your entire life!"

Tali forced her attention away from these thoughts and onto the sign on the door in front of her. A block of polished wood with "Welcome to the Cohen family home!" in cheerful hand-painted letters. It looked like something she'd made in seventh grade. One of the things hiding in the shoebox under her bed.

Sergeant Darom coughed pointedly. Tali swallowed, braced herself, and knocked on the door.

She took a step back, wondering how long it made sense to wait before giving the half-hour ultimatum. She was going over the breaking-in procedure in her mind when the sound of a handle turning startled her. The door pulled wide open, and there was a woman standing there, presumably Talia Cohen, with a wide smile on her face.

"Oh, hello!"

Tali stared at her. She was wearing an orange Gush Katif T-shirt over a three-quarter-sleeve shell and a flowy, layered skirt that fluttered as she moved. A few strands of dark hair poked wildly out from beneath the orange scarf tied around her hair.

The woman peered out past Tali. "Good morning, dear soldiers. You must be so hot standing out there! May I offer you some iced tea?"

In the preceding months, Tali had been prepared for every eventuality. She was ready to withstand verbal and physical abuse of all kinds; she knew how to use a water cannon; she had practiced holding steady in a storage container dangling from a crane, keeping a steady grip on a fighting, full-grown adult. The rigorous "mental preparation" program helped her reframe the hatred that was sure to be spewed at her, helped her conceive of her unit as a gentle, caring adult restraining a wayward child.

But nothing, nothing in the world, had prepared her for Talia Cohen standing on the doorstep and inviting her in for iced tea.

"H-hi," Tali stuttered. "I am Lieutenant Tali Cahana, and I am in charge of the unit that will be escorting you from your home today." It was a well-practiced line, and it came out rushed.

"You are all welcome," Talia said, speaking to the unit at large, "but I don't think this will be necessary. We are just finishing packing up here."

Tali peeked behind the woman into the house. All she could see was a steep staircase and a large houseplant bathing in sunlight from the window.

"Who is in there with you?" she asked.

"Just my children."

Tali glanced at Darom, who was looking at her, waiting for orders. She weighed the circumstances. This woman clearly wasn't going to offer much resistance; she didn't see any infiltrators in there; and it would be a waste to have everybody standing around while Talia packed her family into the car.

Tali cleared her throat. "Darom, take them to the next house and begin the evacuation procedure there. I will stay here to assist Mrs. Cohen." Sergeant Darom nodded and gave the order, and the soldiers broke formation, looking very relieved, and moved on to the next house.

"Do come in. I'm sorry about the mess," Talia said, stepping back into the house as Tali entered.

There were toys and clothes strewn about the tile floor, and half-dressed children were streaking across the living room in peals of laughter. To her left was a spacious kitchen with a large wooden table. A girl with a messy ponytail — probably the eight-year-old — sat at the table, eating a bowl of cereal.

"Emuna," Talia called to her, "will you bring the soldier some iced tea, please?"

The girl dropped her spoon and jumped up, seizing a glass pitcher next to the cereal box. She poured the tea into a plastic cup, spilling a little in her eagerness, and ran up to Tali, handed it to her without a word, and raced back to her cereal. Tali stared at the cup in her hand. The feeling in her stomach reminded her of lifting a pitcher she thought was full, only to discover it was empty. Or stepping onto what she thought was a stair, only to discover that the surface was level.

"I'm sorry," Talia was saying, "what did you say your name was again?"

Tali told her, and Talia's face lit up. "Oh, is that short for Talia?" she grinned.

"No," Tali said, almost too sharply. "Just Tali."

"Ah, okay," Talia said, taking a step back toward the staircase. "Tali. I'm just going upstairs to get the bags. Please make yourself comfortable." She gestured toward the living room, where two little boys were jumping on a large, tired-looking sofa.

Tali's eyes were immediately drawn to the paintings hung across the living room. They all seemed to be painted by the same painter — and they were magnificent. Brilliant colors, flowing lines, intricate detail. Most were of landscapes, but there was one, hanging front and center above the fireplace, that she recognized from the file. It was a painting of the photo of Aharon Cohen, Talia's late husband. Tali turned back toward Talia to ask her about the paintings, but Talia had already disappeared up the stairs.

Tali drifted toward them to get a better look, sipping the iced tea. They were varied landscapes, some of them of the sea, some of the desert, and some of green rolling hills like the ones in the Galilee. The signatures on the lower right corner of each painting answered Tali's question: Talia *Cohen*.

What wouldn't Tali have given to be able to paint like that!

She sank onto the couch, settling into a corner as far away from the boys as possible. She had forgotten about her hydration tank and shifted uncomfortably, leaning forward so it wouldn't squish against her back. The little boys had stopped jumping now and were staring at her.

"Are you the soldier who's going to destroy our house?" one of them asked.

Tali swallowed and shook her head. "I'm just here to help you leave."

"Why?"

Tali just looked at him. Explaining to a child why she was

removing him from his home had not been covered in her training, either.

"That's our father," the other little boy said, pointing at the painting.

Tali was dismayed to discover that there was a lump forming in her throat. "I know."

"The Arabs killed him," the boy continued helpfully.

"I know." Tali swallowed. "I'm sorry," she said.

"He has to move too," he went on, unblinking. "They are going to dig him up and take him to Safed."

Tali dropped her eyes.

"We're moving to Or Haganuz, it's close to where he'll be." With that, he turned and ran off, his sidecurls bouncing, his brother in close pursuit.

Tali heard footsteps on the stairs. Talia emerged from around the corner with a giant backpack, which she lowered to the ground with a grunt.

"Nehorai, Lavi," she called to the boys, "come get your shirts on." Tali watched as Talia struggled to wrestle the children into their clothing. The two-year-old started bawling and Talia had to let go of Lavi to rush over and comfort her. Lavi stripped off the part of the shirt she'd managed to get on him and ran, swinging it over his head and whooping, through the house.

"May I help?" Tali took a step forward.

"Oh, no no," Talia said, lifting the toddler on her hip and shooting a determined smile at Tali as she pursued Lavi. "Sit, sit. You must be tired."

Tali felt an odd guilt at the absurdity of this sentence coming from Talia, who clearly hadn't had a good night's sleep in several years. Tali's parents had gotten divorced when she was six. She remembered her mother scrambling around like this, trying to get her and her brothers dressed and out of the house.

As Talia rushed back and forth between the children, soothing this one, scolding that one, stuffing things into bags, Tali felt something swelling in her chest, a feeling she didn't even really know how to name, but it was becoming deeper and heavier and before she knew it there were tears rolling down her cheeks and she was sobbing, gasping for air, and the room melted into a blur before her.

At first, she thought no one had noticed.

Then she felt sturdy hands on her back.

"Tali... Tali... don't cry.... Emuna, will you bring the soldier a tissue please? ... Tali..."

Talia put her arm around Tali and huddled next to her on the couch. Tali burned with shame, but she couldn't stop the tears any more than she could understand where they were coming from. She felt a tissue being stuffed into her hand, and she quickly blew her nose, struggling to compose herself.

"It's okay... everything's going to be okay..." Talia murmured in her ear. "I know... I know this is hard... it's so hard... it's so hard for everyone..."

Tali lifted her head, looking into the eyes of this woman who had lost everything, who was losing everything, telling her everything was going to be okay.

"All we can do is be kind to each other," Talia said, wiping at her own tears. "This week we read that chapter from Isaiah in synagogue. *Nahamu, nahamu, ami* — be comforted, be comforted, my people.' Comfort each other. That's what He says to do. Nothing makes sense. Nothing will make sense until the Messiah comes. In the meantime, we must comfort each other."

Tali was not sure she believed anything this woman was saying, but in those moments, somehow, it was exactly what she needed to hear.

"But Ima," Emuna piped up, "if the soldier doesn't want to expel us, why can't we stay?"

Talia gazed at her daughter, and Tali saw her jaw harden, but she did not answer.

"I don't want to," Tali said, and she was relieved to hear that her voice was steady and clear. "But it's the right thing to do."

Talia pulled back a little from Tali, giving her an appraising look, and then sighed and turned to her daughter.

"Do you have your bag, Emuna?" she asked.

"Yes."

"But Ima!" One of the boys seemed to have finally realized that they were leaving. He looked up at his mother with wide, watery eyes. "What about the rest of our toys? What about Abba?"

He pointed toward the painting of his father that hung on the wall.

"They will bring me back next week to collect the rest of the things we are taking with us, and I'll come with a big truck." Talia stood up and walked toward the painting. "But we're not leaving him behind."

She reached up and gently took the painting off the wall, holding it for a moment, searching his face. Fresh tears poured down her cheeks.

But Tali's cheeks were dry now. She stood from the couch. "Whenever you're ready," she said, her voice firm.

Talia took the painting to the table, where some brown packing paper was piled, and carefully began to wrap the painting.

"Wait!" Emuna cried out. She ran to the windowsill in the kitchen and grabbed a potted seedling from the shelf. "My plant. Who will take care of it?"

Talia studied her child for a moment and said, "It's probably time it was planted outside anyway."

So Talia went back to wrapping the painting, and Tali escorted Emuna outside to plant the seedling in the garden.

When Emuna was done, Tali took her hand and led her back into the house, where her siblings were gathered around their mother. They looked up at Tali with wide eyes.

Talia hoisted the huge camping backpack onto her back and handed out the little backpacks to the children. She picked up the painting and hugged it to her chest. Then she turned to Tali and drew a deep breath.

"We are ready."

SOLDIERS AT
THE DOOR

The morning of the evacuation, as every morning, Itzik rose before the birds to visit the greenhouses.

His back was too delicate and his joints too arthritic to be of much use on the farm now. But there was an intoxicating atmosphere of concentrated life in the plant nurseries, and ever since his first experiences with farming on kibbutz Kfar Darom, he'd found that energy the perfect antidote for all the death that haunted his nightmares.

Itzik been forced to sell his farm in Katif and move in with his son in Neve Adva after his health made it impossible for him to continue managing on his own. Retirement was not appealing to a man who'd spent every minute of his life fighting for something, but stillness did have its charms. He loved to sit there in the nursery as the sky slowly lightened, watching, breathing in the scent of the moist soil, the greenery, and the dewdrops. When the sun peeked over the horizon, he'd take a stroll through the greenhouse, his hands clasped behind him like a headmaster inspecting his students. Sometimes, he'd stop to finger the outer leaves of a head of lettuce, or sample a cherry tomato. Oh, those tomatoes! He'd never tasted anything like them in Hungary; how they exploded with sweetness in his mouth. "An Israeli innovation!" he exclaimed so often that his grandchildren were well past rolling their eyes and had moved on to selective deafness.

But the last of the crops had already been gathered some time ago. Itzik sat in his usual chair, and stared out over the skeleton of the greenhouse; now just empty soil marked with rows of wooden rods and string.

An image floated into his mind: young men with their shirts tied over their heads, their bare chests brown and muscular, kneeling to inspect the tomato plants. His fists clenched.

Why had Moshe taken those Americans up on their offer to buy the greenhouses and hand them to the Arabs?

As if it weren't enough of a shameful defeat to be handing them this victory. As if it weren't enough to see the home his son had built with his bare hands razed and his neighbors scattered. If they were going to destroy this place, they should destroy everything. Especially the synagogue. He'd heard that some of the synagogues and other public buildings in Gush Katif were to remain standing. This horrified him. There was no telling what the savages might do, and he had already seen more than his share of Jewish houses of prayer being sacked and burned to the ground by Jew-hating mobs.

The heat was suffocating, though the sun had barely risen; but there was a cold in Itzik's bones that morning, and he shivered.

As he made his way back toward the house, he spotted something on the hill beyond the barbed wire fence — a little Arab girl in a pink dress, sitting with her knees hugged to her chest. He paused, considering whether he should report this to security, but decided against it. Something about her posture made him feel a twinge of pity, and after all, she was just a little girl.

He entered the kitchen, turned on the electric kettle, and lowered himself into the chair by the kitchen table with a grunt. The years of farm work had kept his bones strong and his spine straight, and he was grateful that he could move with ease compared to others his age. But his wrists and fingers always hurt the most in the morning. He prepared a mug of sweet tea and held it for a long time before drinking, staring at the numbers on his arm.

The nightmares had faded somewhat over the years, but they'd started coming back in the last few months. He'd wake up in a cold sweat, shaking and yelling in Hungarian, and his son would appear before him in the dark, silently stroking his head until he calmed. He couldn't remember most of the dreams by morning; just snippets of sensations. The suffocating squeeze and the gentle rocking of the trains. The burn of the whip on his back. The horrible, stomach-turning stench from the crematoria.

But the dream last night had been so vividly detailed. The first part, at least, seemed to be dredged up, intact, from the depths of his memory. The clink of silverware. The aroma of his mother's beef stew. The pounding on the door. The look of sheer terror his parents exchanged. His older brother Joel reaching for the handle. His father's voice: *"Don't!"*

Shouts in a language he didn't understand, heavy boots kicking over chairs, his mother's whimpers. Stumbling out onto the cobblestone street. Being thrown to the ground by the SS officer for not walking fast enough. The impact of the boot on his stomach, the clench of breathless pain. Joel's voice, "Leave him alone." The single shot echoing through the streets. His mother's wail, the crack of the butt of a pistol against her skull as the officer screamed at her to shut up and get in the truck. Pushed into a dark space. Feeling for something in the dark. A door. The front door. In Neve Adva. More knocks, more shouts. He backed away, stumbling over chairs. But Moshe was there, reaching for the door handle. Itzik wanted to shout for him to stop but no sound would come out. He watched helplessly as Moshe opened the door.

And there, standing in the doorway, was Joel. Alive. Sandy brown hair. Twinkling hazel eyes. Still in his half-buttoned coat. Laughing. Loud, raucous laughter that Itzik hadn't heard in sixty years. "It's me," he was saying. "It's just me."

"Abba, what's wrong?"

Itzik started and looked up, snapping back to reality. Moshe was standing there in his sleeveless undershirt, his beard wild, his forehead wrinkled in concern. That was when Itzik felt the wetness on his cheeks.

"Nothing," he said, wiping the tears away with his hand. "Bad dream last night."

"Again?" Moshe peeked into the kettle. He opened the lid and shoved it under the faucet to top it off. "I'm not surprised." He clunked the kettle onto its electronic cradle and flicked the switch. He sat down and took his father's hand. "Soon this will all be over."

They sat in silence, waiting for the water to boil.

Usually, after tea, Moshe would go out to the greenhouses to tend to the plants and oversee the labor. Bruria would sit at the sewing machine patching together quilts out of scraps of used cloth. But today they sat in the living room in dismal silence, deep in their own thoughts. They hadn't packed anything; they didn't intend to. But there seemed to be little point in trying to create or plant something new.

Finally Bruria stood from the armchair.

"I can't just sit here," she said.

"What do you intend to do?" Moshe asked her.

"I don't know, I don't know, what am I supposed to do?" She paced the rug. "What am I supposed to not do? There is no point in going anywhere, there is no point in staying. They will be here in an hour. That's no time at all. And it's an eternity. I can't just sit here for another hour. Maybe I should just…" Her voice trailed off as her eyes rested on her father-in-law. He looked back at her wearily. The suggestion hung in the air for a few moments, until Itzik finally went ahead and said it.

"Pack?"

Bruria's face scrunched up and she covered her mouth with her hand, a lock of graying brown hair falling forward over her face. Moshe was at her side before she emitted her first sob, and then she crumpled to the floor, and he with her.

"How can they do this to us?" Her voice came out muffled from under her hand. "How dare they come here and throw your father out of his home!"

Bruria, too, was a child of survivors. She had also grown up with ghosts in the house, and with an inherited edginess around sudden movements and loud sounds. Itzik hated spending time with her parents when they were still around, because none of them wanted to talk about it, but all of them wanted to talk about it, but no one dared bring it up.

"Well," Itzik said, "if we are planning to have guests in an hour, perhaps we should prepare to receive them."

Bruria looked up at him, her eyes red and confused. "What do you mean?" she asked. "You want me to serve them lemonade?"

"They should understand what they are doing. Let's get out the photo albums," he said, pointing to the bookshelf. "We can show them the life we have lived here and what they are taking us away from. And I will show them this," he tapped the inside of his forearm, "and let them know that this is the second time I have been thrown out of my home."

"I'm not sure I can bear to look at the photos," Bruria said, sitting back and rubbing her eyes.

"We've only been here twelve years anyway," Moshe said softly. "Dror was already nine when we moved down here. How old was Adi?"

"Six."

"Six. It's not like this is the only home they ever knew."

"I wanted to die here," Bruria said, looking out the window that faced the sea. "I wanted to grow old listening to the sound of those waves."

Itzik followed her gaze. He had wanted to die here, too.

"You won't fight them, will you, Abba?" Bruria sent a sharp look in Itzik's direction. "Don't make them carry you. Please."

"I am not setting foot out of this house of my own volition. I didn't sneak onto Palmahim Beach and fight three wars so I could be evicted from my house by another Jew."

"Abba," Bruria started to scold him, but Moshe touched her arm and gave his head a little shake. She sighed, and then stood up with several grunts.

"I'm going to make breakfast."

She disappeared into the kitchen. Moshe watched her leave, then turned to his father.

"She is worried you will get hurt."

"I know."

"So am I."

"I know."

"I don't know if they will be gentle."

"I don't care."

"Maybe we could talk to them."

Itzik snorted. "Yes. Like we could talk to the government."

"Do you have to make them throw you out of here like an animal?" Moshe's gaze went hard. "It's going to happen, one way or the other. I know we don't want to say it. None of us have wanted to say it. I'm tired of not saying things. Can't we just go gently?"

"No!" Itzik felt his blood rushing to his face. "I will not go gently! I would rather they drag my dead body out of here than walk with them willingly! I will not be intimidated! Those days are over, boy!"

Moshe was wincing, but he was used to these outbursts. He heaved a sigh and stood up from the floor, and then silently went after Bruria, leaving Itzik in his chair with his fists clenched and his jaw set.

Itzik sat there a few moments, stiff with anger; but then his eyes locked on to the old portrait on the bookshelf across the room, and everything softened. Ruti's kind eyes and bright smile always unburdened him a little. She was a sabra, born on the kibbutz where Itzik had settled after making aliyah. From the moment he laid eyes on her — even though he couldn't speak a word of her language — he sought her presence at every opportunity. She walked with a lightness in her step, and her laughter reminded him of the symphony of birdsong during sunrise, and it came more easily to her than to anyone else he knew, even while she was fading from illness. His heart clenched in pain every time he thought of her, but at the same time, it lifted from the light and joy she had brought into his otherwise haunted life. He still felt that, twenty years after her death. This faded sepia print, taken when she was in her thirties, somehow encapsulated that light. The picture had been sitting like a lantern on the shelf since they had moved here.

Itzik pushed himself out of the chair and crossed the room, studying her face. What would she have said to do about the soldiers? Would she have cooked them breakfast, too?

Probably.

He picked up the portrait and pressed it to his lips, and then turned to join his son and daughter-in-law in the kitchen.

———❧———

They were finishing their omelets when the knock at the door came. Bruria froze, her eyes fixed on her plate. Moshe pursed his lips and set down his fork. Itzik narrowed his eyes at the door.

Another knock. "Skolnik family," came a voice. "Please open the door."

None of them moved.

Then Itzik pushed himself out of his chair with surprising speed, startling Moshe and Bruria. He shoved his plate to the middle of the table.

"Who's there?" he called. "Who has come to throw an old Holocaust survivor out of his house again?" He started for the door.

"Abba, no." Bruria caught his arm, but he pulled away.

"Let me show them." He made his way toward the door, turned the handle, and pulled it open, ready to unleash his wrath on whoever stood there. But as soon as he laid eyes on the soldier in the doorway, his hands went limp and the blood drained from his face.

That sandy brown hair. Those hazel eyes. The dimple in the soldier's chin. The slope of his shoulders.... It was his brother's spitting image.

"*Joel*," Itzik rasped.

Moshe leapt up from his chair to rush to his father's side. The soldier blinked, disoriented, but quickly regained composure.

"Good morning," he said, "I am Sergeant Yoel Darom, and I'll be escorting you from your home today."

Itzik let out a faint cry, and fell forward into the startled sergeant's arms.

THE MEMORY
OF RAIN

Peduel spat on the ground next to the Malul family's welcome mat and wiped a bead of sweat from his brow. He glanced at his watch again. 9:32 AM. He and his unit had been standing here since 8:30.

"Nu, how much longer?" he muttered under his breath, earning him a glare from his commanding officer.

He shifted his weight from one foot to the other, staring at the ground. He was boiling inside and out.

Ayala had responded to his text message a few months before with a quick, "Understood. Good luck" and a smiley face. Though he did not hear from her at all in the months that followed, her mysterious smile haunted him throughout his training and preparation for the disengagement, and every time he thought of her, his fists clenched. Eventually, after practicing a series of scenarios where the guys playing the settlers had been a little too convincing, he had asked his commander to assign him to the "third circle" — the group of soldiers responsible for securing the settlements from outside threats, who wouldn't need to interact with the settlers. On the morning of August 15th, as he climbed on the transport that would take him to his first mission, his phone had buzzed: "Good luck today." Smiley face.

Over the past two days he had composed a thousand nasty replies in his head, but he'd been too busy securing perimeters and scouting for infiltrators to actually type any of them on his phone. Then, on the morning of the 18th, Lieutenant Hershko informed him that he was needed in the "first circle" for the evacuation of Neve Adva, to replace one of the soldiers who had had enough. Peduel had understood that this was likely to happen, but he still had to force out his "yes, sir" through gritted teeth.

"All right." Lieutenant Hersho's voice snapped him back to reality. "Let's get this over with. Commence break-in procedure."

Within a few minutes, Peduel was shuffling into the hallway of the house with four other team members. It had been many years since he had set foot in the house of a religious family, and he found his eyes sweeping the hallway and the adjacent rooms, looking for familiarity. The whitewash on the walls was scuffed and stained from wayward shoe soles and sticky fingers; his mother would never have tolerated such a thing. The cramped kitchen off to the right was piled high with dirty dishes, and there was no assembly line of little sisters scrubbing them. On the wall opposite him, at the end of the hallway, hung an embroidered cloth that read, "*May God bless you and keep you.*" The first line of the Priestly Blessing.

He knew that blessing by heart. His father was a Cohen, and every Shabbat morning during Peduel's childhood, he steered Peduel to the front of the room with the other Cohanim. He would tuck Peduel under his woolen prayer shawl as they blessed the congregation. Peduel would peek out from the shawl to see the whole synagogue standing there with their heads bowed. They were not allowed to look up. Peduel would glance up at his father, whose eyes were closed in concentration, and shiver with the thrilling danger — and creeping loneliness — of being the only person in the room with his eyes open during these most holy moments of the prayer service.

Peduel looked away from the wall hanging and set his jaw. The last thing he'd been expecting to feel right now was an overwhelming longing to be tucked under that prayer shawl one more time.

Yacov Malul was sitting on a couch of faded red fabric, staring straight ahead at the wall opposite him. He was a tall, thin man with a neatly trimmed beard and a large kippa on his head. A young boy was seated next to him, and a little girl clung to his leg, both staring up at the soldiers. The floor was littered with Duplos and plastic dinosaurs. Somewhere down the hall, a toddler was whining.

"Good morning, Mr. Malul," Hershko said.

"A morning of light," Malul replied without looking up.

"Do you mind if we take a seat?"

"Please."

Hershko sat in the armchair next to the couch and started playing therapist, listening as Malul started ranting at him about the mission of the Jewish people and the sacrifices of living in Neve Adva and what a crime against humanity it was to hand their homes to their murderous neighbors. Peduel backed into a corner of the room as the other soldiers became engaged in the conversation. *Idiots*, he thought. *There's no talking to these people.*

A movement at the entrance to the room caught his eye. It was a woman with a toddler on her hip and a swollen belly, her hair wrapped in a scarf of blazing orange. She squeezed in next to the child on the couch, and when she looked up, Peduel's breath caught in his chest.

Naama.

Those emerald-green eyes so striking against her deeply tanned skin. The black curl peeking out from underneath the scarf. The high cheekbones. There was no mistaking her. How had he not recognized her in the photographs Hershko had showed them before the evacuation? But then, photographs had never quite done her justice. Age had added some worry lines to her forehead; motherhood had made her swollen in some places and softer in others, and added dark circles under her eyes; but to Peduel, these changes only served to enhance her beauty. He had first noticed her outside the synagogue in Elon Moreh, sitting on a bench facing the valley with the wind blowing her hair softly around her face. He had been thirteen; she had been twelve. Her family had just moved to the settlement. She had turned around to look at him with those piercing green eyes, and his knees had gone rubbery.

He was astonished and dismayed to discover that his knees were doing exactly that now. He leaned against a nearby book-case to steady himself. She didn't see him; she was frowning at Hershko, listening to his verbal sparring match with her husband. Peduel couldn't understand what was happening to him. It had been ten years. He thought he'd moved on, he thought he had grieved her with the rest of his losses, he had dated and fallen in and out of love since. And here he was, in this house in Neve Adva, and just one look at her exquisite face made it all come crashing down on him again. The three years that were the worst and the best in his life. The months he spent being afraid to talk to her. That activity at the Bnei Akiva youth group that had forced them into conversation. The night they agreed that they would marry when they were old enough. The day his mother found out, and grudgingly gave permission for Peduel to continue seeing her.

The voices around him slurred together as though underwater. All other sights went blurry. There was nothing in that room but him, his pounding heart, and her.

The tassels on her scarf reminded him of the way her hair hung when it was wet, and that brought back another vivid memory: that time, just a few months before everything fell apart, when they had snuck out late one Friday night and been caught in a sudden storm. They ran to find shelter and ducked into a covered bus stop by the road. Her hair was dripping and she was shivering. He had reached a trembling hand toward her, to tuck a stray curl behind her ear. She had ducked away from him, giggling nervously.

"Peduel!"

"Oh, Naama," he said. "What harm could it do?"

"It could ruin everything. No touching until the wedding. My parents will never let us stay together if they hear you're not keeping that law."

"They don't have to know," he whispered, reaching again for her face, and for one glorious moment, she held still, her eyes closed, not breathing, as his fingers lightly brushed against her cheek. Then she jumped from her chair and ran back out into the rain, and he sat there, afraid to touch anything or move his hand lest the magic sensation of her skin dissolve from his fingertips.

He had touched several women in the ten years that had passed since then, even slept with a few, and yet nothing ever came close to the intimacy of that moment with Naama.

Losing her had been the worst part of leaving his life in Elon Moreh behind. His anger at his parents for expelling him for what felt like such a stupid and backward reason protected him from the grief of losing them, at least for a while. But Naama? He never had the chance to say goodbye. He thought of her every moment of every day for the first year. Every time he passed a young woman with dark hair and tan skin on the street his heart raced with the thought that it might be her — and then broke all over again when he rushed to get a closer look and realized it wasn't. During the worst nights, he would close his eyes and grit his teeth and think of her, of her shy smile, of her gentle laugh, of the way she absently traced her bottom lip when she was thinking. He had thought about sending her a letter to explain everything and apologize, but in the fog of trying to survive and get himself off the street, he never got around to it.

He was trembling all over and to his horror, he felt a tear escape the corner of his eye. He wiped it away quickly and tried to breathe and refocus on Malul and Hershko — and that's when he saw that they were crying, too. In fact, everyone in the room was crying. He had no idea why, but it didn't matter — now he could cry openly and no one would look at him sideways. So he let himself weep as Malul and Hershko stood up and embraced each other and the female soldier took the toddler from Naama.

Then Naama turned toward him and her eyes met his.

She gasped, and her hand flew to her mouth. The rest of the room seemed to fade away again, and for several heartbeats, they stood there staring at each other, not daring to breathe.

"Peduel?" she finally said, drifting toward him like a ghost. One of her hands clutched her chest; the other rested on her pregnant belly. "Is that really you?"

Peduel found himself completely unable to speak. The grief he felt now mingled with sparks of joy that she recognized and remembered him, and he found himself laughing through his tears, nodding.

"I don't believe it," Naama breathed. "After all these years…"

"You know him?" Her husband's voice seemed to break the spell, letting all the noise and chaos around them come rushing in.

"Oh, I…I did," Naama said, looking flustered, her face flushing. "He's a…he's an old friend." Her eyes locked back onto Peduel's. "How have you…how have you been?"

Peduel took a few moments to find his tongue. "I…I'm doing okay now," he said. "It was…hard for a while. I wanted to write to you…"

"I wanted…I tried…" She shot an apprehensive look at her husband, who was picking up one of the kids to carry to the door. She cleared her throat. "Anyway. It's…so good to see you."

Peduel was unable to respond, and she broke eye contact and turned around, sweeping out of the room. He tried to follow her but found himself crashing into another soldier and almost tripping over a kid. When he finally managed to push past everyone and leave the house, he saw her bent over the back seat, buckling the toddler in. Then she stood, and turned back toward the house, and their eyes locked again. She froze, and for a moment neither of them moved.

"Naama," her husband called from the front seat, and she snapped out of it, shaking her head a little and nodding at Peduel, looking like she wanted to say something polite but couldn't think of anything to say. Then she lowered her eyes again and walked around the car to the passenger's seat. Peduel just stood there, numb, as she shot one last glance in his direction and the car pulled away.

All at once, a thousand memories crashed down on him. The weight of his father's hands on his head as he blessed him on Friday nights, his beautiful baritone voice singing the *Kiddush*. The warmth of his mother's embrace, the smell of her perfume as he dug his face into her shoulder, her hand gently stroking his head as her sleeves soaked up his tears. The laughter of his little sisters playing hide-and-seek in the backyard. The light in his parents' eyes when he read to them from the Torah for the first time; the beaming face of his father when Peduel stood on the *bimah* and read the Torah for his bar mitzvah. The mouth-watering aroma of his mother's Friday night chicken soup. The feeling of his father's hand on his cheek, and the sound of his voice whispering, *I love you, son. I'm so proud of you.*

The images swam before his eyes in such a dizzying, vivid display that he didn't even notice that he had sunk to his knees until Lieutenant Hershko's hand came down firm on his shoulder.

"Katz! What's wrong? Someone call a medic over here!"

Peduel was escorted to the ambulance crew, and they fussed over him, taking his pulse, making him drink. Eventually they concluded that he didn't need an IV, but told Hershko he should be dismissed from duty.

And so Peduel found himself on the bus back to Tel Aviv that afternoon. He leaned back against the threadbare headrest, and was just at the edge of falling asleep when his phone buzzed again. Annoyed, he drew it out.

How's it going?

Peduel stared at his phone for a long time.

Finally, he tapped out:

Nightmare. They dismissed me. On the bus back to Tel Aviv now. Are you home?

Send.

He waited, holding his breath, feeling a little giddy.

Sorry to hear it. I'll be home after work. You want to come over? Feel free any time after seven.

———⁓∾⁓———

At 7:05 he pulled open the glass door where Ayala had disappeared months before and trotted up two flights of stairs. He raised his fist and paused a moment before knocking on the door. It swung open, and there she was with that same mysterious smile playing at the corners of her well-defined lips. She looked him up and down, her eyes gleaming.

"You look good in uniform," she said, stepping aside and gesturing for him to come inside. He did so, perplexed by the warmth that rose in his belly from her compliment. Ayala's apartment was very much like his: cramped, and furnished with Ikea couches, an old bookcase stuffed far beyond capacity, and a small, worn table with two plastic chairs. She, at least, had bothered with a little décor: a vase here, a throw pillow there, and a few family photographs on the wall. She shut the door behind him.

"So," she said. "How can I help you, Peduel?"

He turned to face her. She was wearing a low-cut black blouse, the bleached ends of her hair spilling toward the plunging neckline. Up until that moment, he'd had no idea what the answer to that question would be. After months of being furious with her, he'd astonished himself by even showing up on her doorstep. But before he fully grasped what he was doing, he leaned in, grabbed her waist, and kissed her hungrily. She responded at first with surprise and then with enthusiasm, circling her arms around his shoulders. As his lips drifted downward to explore the hollow of her neck, he felt her laughing softly.

"Okay then," she murmured into his hair.

Later, as he lay there on Ayala's bed with her head resting in the crook of his arm, everything spilled out of him in a babbling gush: the memories, the tears, the anger, the sadness, the doubt. He told her about Naama and that night under the bus stop, and about what it felt like to watch her drive away as every warm and happy memory from his childhood accosted him at once. Ayala listened, absently tracing patterns on his bare chest with her fingertips. When the flow of words and tears slowed to a trickle and petered out, she spread her hand flat over his heart, and they both lay there, feeling it beat.

"You know, Peduel..." Ayala began slowly. "There are things...there are things we left behind in that world that are beautiful beyond words. That moment you describe with Naama...it's not something you will ever be able to recreate in the world you and I occupy now. The power of that touch was made possible by all the forbiddenness around it. That doesn't mean you'll never experience happiness." She paused. "There is nothing any of us wants more than daddy's approval, no matter how cruel he was to you or how much you've told yourself you hated him over all these years. You miss them," she went on, reaching up to wipe a fresh wave of tears flowing from his eyes. "You're allowed to miss them. You're supposed to miss them. If you didn't want their love, you wouldn't be human."

"But all the choices I've made have shut me out of receiving that love. Forever."

"At the end of the day, you had to choose between being true to yourself and continuing to live a lie just to have their love. You know you made the right choice. That doesn't mean you're not allowed to mourn what you walked away from."

Peduel rubbed fiercely at his eyes. "You sound like my therapist again."

Ayala laughed, propping herself up on her elbow, her hair spilling over Peduel's chest. "Clearly," she said, "she shirked her duties, and I am forced to pick up where she left off."

"Well, if this is supposed to be the next stage of therapy, I'm definitely glad you took over." He smiled, reaching over and running a hand down her back. Ayala giggled and leaned over to kiss him again. Then she sat up.

"Want to get dinner?" she said, reaching for her blouse and pulling it over her head. "Fettuccini with salsa rosa?" she teased.

"You know..." He sat up and wrapped his arms around her waist, burying his face into her shoulder, inhaling her scent. "Maybe I'll try something else this time. Any suggestions?"

KISSUFIM

Reuben sat in the parked car, staring dismally at the front door, for a good few minutes before stepping out.

He heard the yelling and crying before he even got to the steps. He knew what he would find: toys everywhere, a spaghetti-encrusted kitchen floor, his hyperactive seven-year-old streaking through the house in his underwear, the two-year-old throwing a tantrum someplace, and his wife, her hair frizzy from the humidity and eyes dark-rimmed and empty, sitting listlessly on the couch, too depressed to care.

This picture hadn't been on the Nefesh B'Nefesh pamphlet, that's for sure.

He turned the handle and pulled the door open slowly and tentatively, in an effort to avoid announcing his presence. Maybe if he was quiet enough, he could slip into the office and wait for a lull in the chaos before greeting Shelly. But she spotted him before he had closed the door behind him.

"Oh thank *God*," she growled, standing up from the couch. "Please take over in here before I murder your children."

And with that she marched up the stairs to the bedroom.

After soothing Shira and bribing Daniel into his pants, he dragged the two of them out to the neighborhood playground. At six in the evening, the air was still heavy with humidity, but at least the sun wasn't quite as oppressive as it had been earlier.

Reuben set Daniel loose on the jungle gym and tried to talk Shira into riding on the bouncy horse. She finally found a pile of pebbles to entertain herself, and Reuben sank onto a nearby bench, resting his forehead in his hands.

Other parents were mulling around, chatting with each other. He didn't even try to make out what they were saying. After a year in Israel he was able to make basic conversation, buy groceries, order pizza. He was a pro at ordering pizza at this point. But the fact that he worked in overseas sales, in an entirely English-speaking environment, significantly hindered his progress in picking up the language. Just hearing the rapid-fire speech of his neighbors was exhausting.

He felt a sharp clap on the back.

"Ruby! How'z eet goeeng?"

Reuben looked up. His Moroccan-Israeli neighbor, Tzahi, was grinning widely down at him. Like many Israelis, Tzahi always preferred to speak to him in heavily accented broken English instead of letting Reuben practice his Hebrew. Reuben didn't know what to do with what was apparently the Israeli diminutive for his name.

Tzahi sat down next to him, shaking his head. "Crazy, crazy," he was saying. "Dees country, eez a crazy place."

Reuben tried to draw the corners of his mouth up into a grin as he nodded. Tzahi constantly asked him why he left behind his comfortable life in America to come to Israel. At first Reuben had tried to explain to him about the Zionist dream, about the meaning of an ancestral homeland and why it was worth the sacrifice, about what it would mean to his Holocaust survivor grandparents to have their great-grandson serve in a Jewish army — and about Shelly and Nava Applebaum. But Tzahi always just shook his head and clicked his tongue.

On days like these, Reuben really had no answer for him.

"You see on da televizia?" Tzahi was asking him.

"See what?" Reuben asked, distracted by a cry that turned out to be from a child who wasn't his.

"Da...nu...da *hitnatkut?* Taking da *mitnahlim* from Aza?" He mimed shoving something with his hands. He shook his head again. "Don't know what weel be wees dees. I woz for eet, but now not so shoor."

Reuben had only a vague idea what he was saying, but he kept nodding. There was another cry, and this time he was pretty sure it was Shira.

"*Sliha,*" he apologized to Tzahi. "*Habat sheli.*"

"No problem," Tzahi said and clapped him on the shoulder again. "She should be healsy!"

He let the kids play for an hour or so, and then dragged them back to the house to feed them and get them ready for bed. Shelly was still in the bedroom when he got back. Probably napping. It was just as well.

He scraped the spaghetti off the floor, swept the toys into a corner, made toast and omelets, took out the trash. Filled the bathtub. Washed the kids. Sat them in front of the TV as he struggled to read the letter from Daniel's school in the pile of mail. He gave up in the middle, resting his forehead on the table, feeling exhausted and incompetent and helpless. School would begin in another few weeks, and Shelly would have to flounder through the parent-teacher meetings. At least having the kids out of the house and being able to go back to work might help her feel less depressed.

You mean the work where she has to help kids improve their speech skills in a language she hardly speaks herself? he asked himself wryly.

He glanced up the stairs, feeling a pang of worry. He hadn't remembered her being like this since the postpartum depression after Daniel was born. But if he brought up therapy, she'd probably lose it at him.

By the grace of God, Shira fell asleep on the couch and Reuben carried her up to her crib. Daniel was a tougher customer. Reuben read him three stories and sang him seven songs before he was willing to accept his good-night kiss.

Reuben stumbled down the stairs and started clearing the table from dinner, snacking on his children's cold leftover eggs as he loaded the dishwasher. Then he poured himself a generous glass of scotch. He eyed the near-empty bottle with concern. He'd have to ask around to see if anyone was coming back from the USA soon and could pick up some for him at duty-free. Alcoholic beverages were unreasonably expensive in Israel. This was not something he had to worry about before he made aliyah.

There was a lot he didn't have to worry about before he made aliyah.

Finally, with a huge sigh of relief, Reuben sank into his easy chair and closed his eyes, reveling in the silence.

Not twenty seconds passed before the phone rang.

He stared at it ruefully from across the room, letting it ring three or four times before getting up to answer it.

"Hello?"

"Hi, honey."

"Mom! Hi," Reuben said, trying to work up the energy to sound happy to hear her voice.

"How are you guys?"

Reuben cast a look around the room, at the toys piled in the corner, at the dining room table piled high with kids' drawings and junk mail, at the dishwasher full of dishes, at the ever-growing Mt. Laundry near the laundry room under the stairs.

"Fine," he said.

His mother started chattering about this and that, about the multimillion dollar deal his brother had just signed, about the latest gadget his father was excited about, about the Red Sox game she'd taken his sister's kids to, about the gossip from Reuben's aunts. He went back to his chair and sat down, the phone tucked between his ear and his shoulder, trying to throw in the occasional grunt to assure her he was still there. As the conversation came to a close, she asked him, for the ten millionth time, if he was sure he had made the right decision, and for the ten millionth time, he firmly lied that yes, he was sure.

"We just miss you so much here," his mother said, her voice breaking a little. Reuben clutched his glass, his knuckles turning white. "Things just aren't the same without you. I worry about you every day."

When they hung up, he let out a slow breath and gulped down the last of his scotch. He set the glass on the coffee table, and then reached for the remote and switched on the TV.

Oh, right. The disengagement. That's probably what Tzahi was babbling about earlier.

Onscreen, a reporter was broadcasting from Kissufim Checkpoint, the crossing point from Israel proper to Gaza. A mess of buses, soldiers, and media crews swarmed behind him.

Reuben had had more urgent things to focus on than the news about the withdrawal from Gaza. His awareness of the flow of events was vague. But lunch hour discussions at work taught him rather quickly that you can't live in Israel for five minutes without having an opinion on politics. He was undecided on the move itself — he saw advantages and disadvantages — but despite identifying as a religious Zionist himself, the settlers annoyed the hell out of him. He couldn't even understand what they were wailing in those clips from the protests, but their emotionalism made the muscles in his temples twitch. He watched with growing irritation, and for once it wasn't because he couldn't understand the Hebrew. Onscreen, IDF soldiers were solemnly taking hold of grown men and women and dragging them physically onto buses. Why couldn't the settlers just grow up and face the government's decision with dignity? Didn't they realize they'd lost the fight long ago?

He kept watching, his mind swimming with the images of orange-clad teenagers wriggling in the arms of soldiers, until his eyelids grew heavy, and the remote slid from his hand...

A gurgle of water. Reuben opened his eyes. He was sitting in the grass by a pond with a little fountain. *The* pond. The pond in the park a couple blocks from his house in Boston, where he spent Saturday afternoons with the family. He looked up. There was his wife in a sunhat, laughing, chasing Daniel with Shira in the baby backpack. He stared at Shelly, mesmerized. It had been months since he'd seen her laugh.

She was chasing Daniel and moving further away from him, and he stood up to follow them, but they were moving fast and he started to run, trying to catch them.

"Shelly, wait!" he called, but they disappeared into a thicket of trees. When he finally reached it himself, he entered and found himself on the sidewalk on his old street in Boston. His house was just a few blocks down the road. He looked around him, and noticed that something was wrong. The houses were not in the right order. It was like all the houses of all his loved ones had moved onto the same street. There was his childhood home in Columbus. Next to it was the house of his best friend growing up. Next was the house Shelly lived in before they got married.

His chest started to swell with this feeling, a feeling that has no words in English.

But there was a word. A word in Portuguese. Shelly mentioned it the other day. She'd been sorting through pictures from previous summers in Boston, and she'd described what she felt with this word.

Somehow it became very important that he remember.

What was the word?

He walked past the lawns, and the unnamed feeling grew, mixed with a sort of dread that something terrible was happening. There was total silence and not a soul was in sight. He stopped in front of his parents' house, peering under the awning. The windchimes jangled softly, and the colored paper mobile made by one of his nephews twirled lazily in the breeze.

"Mom? Dad?"

A loud rumble startled him and he turned around. A bulldozer was charging up the street. His heart pounded in fear. He tried to run but his feet wouldn't move, and he watched in terror as the bulldozer drove straight for him. With the scoop just a few feet away, it suddenly turned and ran over the picket fence surrounding his parents' house.

"What are you doing?" he yelled. The bulldozer charged at the house and ran right into it and the house just crumbled to the ground.

"Stop!"

His feet could move again and he sprinted toward the house next to the one that had just turned to dust. It was the house he recognized as his own, the house he and Shelly had lived in for eight years before they made aliyah. The bench swing, the one that used to be at their parents' house, the one where they were sitting when he proposed to her, was rocking gently back and forth on the front porch.

The bulldozer had turned and was now aiming straight for it.

"No! No!" he screamed, but the bulldozer didn't stop, and soon his home, too, was a pile of rubble.

The noise was deafening, and he looked around him in horror to see bulldozers everywhere, razing the houses of all his memories, all his loved ones, everything he had had to leave behind.

Above the din of destruction, a voice was singing. His rabbi from the synagogue. He was singing a line from the Friday night services. *"Ki zeh kama nikhsof nikhsafti* — for so long I have yearned..."

That was the word! Reuben suddenly realized. Not in Portuguese, but in Hebrew.

Kissufim.

Unspeakable longing.

There was a clap on his back.

"Ruby!"

Reuben turned around to see Tzahi behind him.

"Tzahi!" he shouted. "We have to stop them!"

"No, no," Tzahi yelled over the noise of the bulldozers. *"Kissufim!* We need to get to Kissufim Checkpoint!"

"What are you talking about?!"

"Reuben!" Now Tzahi's voice sounded like Shelly's. "Reuben!"

―⁕―

"Reuben!" Reuben jerked awake, gasping. He was drenched in cold sweat, hyperventilating, his hands shaking. Shelly's face was in front of him. She was squinting in the light of the living room, clutching her robe closed, her hair a wild auburn cloud around her face.

"Oh my God," Reuben panted.

"Are you okay? You were yelling," Shelly said.

Reuben looked around him, disoriented, and his eyes locked onto the television screen. It was still on, and this time it was playing the English language news.

" — and here we see the bus from Neve Adva crossing Kissufim Checkpoint, the last to leave the Gaza Strip this evening," the announcer was saying, as a big purple and white bus pulled in in front of the camera. The face of a teenager with a dark complexion appeared in the window of a bus, then disappeared, and was replaced by an arm tossing something to the side of the road. The image switched to more of the footage Reuben had seen earlier. Settlers being led away from houses, sobbing and yelling. "The settlement was evacuated with relatively little resistance, though we have a report of a soldier who passed out, apparently from dehydration."

Shelly pointed the remote at the TV and switched it off.

Reuben wiped his brow.

"Too much TV," he said.

Shelly watched as he shakily pulled himself to his feet.

"Reuben," she murmured. "Are you okay?"

He looked at her for a moment, then pulled her into a hug.

"I'm okay," he said. "I'll be okay." A tear escaped the corner of his eye, and he held Shelly close, hoping she wouldn't see it. "I just miss home."

"Me too," she whispered. "God, me too."

EROSION

On the morning of August 18th, 2005, Benny Borokhov was rudely awakened by the sound of his mother throwing open the shades in his bedroom, and the sudden glare of harsh sunlight streaming onto his face.

"Mama," he moaned, covering his face with his elbow to seal his eyes in darkness again.

"We're going on a hike," came his mother's clipped voice. He heard Levana squirming and groaning on the other side of the room, and his mother's footsteps crossing back toward the door.

"Anyone who is dressed and at the breakfast table in ten minutes or less is getting a *shoko*," Mama tossed over her shoulder.

Ten minutes later, Benny was sandwiched between his sisters at the table, all three of them sucking on the corners of their bags of chocolate milk. Twelve-year-old Kinneret was slouched over the table, her strawberry blond curls drooping over her face. Eight-year-old Levana cast an animated look across the living room and spotted something the other two hadn't noticed.

She pointed at the television. "Why is the little light off?" she asked.

Mama, who was tossing hummus-and-pickle sandwiches into a backpack, took a few moments to answer.

"No TV today," she said, and raised her hand against the wave of protest that rose from the children. "We are going on a hike and we're staying out all day. I don't want to be anywhere near a television or a radio."

"But it's so hot!" whined Levana.

"You'll live. If you're good, we'll get popsicles at Rosh Hanikra, and find a sandy spot on the beach."

"But why do we have to do this today?" Benny asked.

"Because of the disengagement, stupid," Kinneret snapped at him.

"Quiet," Olga said, and the kids slouched over their *shokos* again and didn't say another word.

After breakfast, the four of them set out on the road from Betzet toward the coast. Benny felt sweat begin to run down his back before they had even turned the corner of their street. The summers in Neve Adva had been so much hotter, despite the breeze that blew off the same sea; but August was still brutal in Betzet, and before long he noticed that Kinneret's skin was nearing the color of her hair. He studied the back of his mother's neck, shaded by her wide-brimmed sunhat, to see if her complexion was the same shade. He still wasn't used to being able to see the back of her neck. One day shortly after the move to Betzet, he and Levana had come home from school to discover that their mother had chopped her hair startlingly short; for as long as he could remember she'd had long, flowing strawberry-blonde tresses, but there she was in the kitchen, sipping tea and sporting a practical bob. Benny hardly recognized her at first. Levana had been so shocked that she'd burst into tears. They got used to it after a little while, but Benny noticed something odd about the look on Mama's face when he caught her glancing at her reflection in the mirror — a sort of stubborn triumph.

The family walked along the beach until they reached the mountain on the border with Lebanon, and then they took the cable car down to see the grottos. As they approached the entrance to the caves, Kinneret announced that she was not going in, because she had been there three times already and it was boring. Benny steeled himself for a stern lecture from their mother about wasting their entrance fee, but she just gave a dismissive sort of growl and turned into the cave. Benny and Levana followed her.

The grottos of Rosh Hanikra were the best thing about living in Betzet. Benny loved tiptoeing through the caverns, pretending he was a Maccabee hiding from the Greeks, or an Etzel fighter hiding from the British, like the ones who blew up the bridge depicted in the movie the site played for tourists. He liked to find a quiet corner along the trail in the caves, sit down, close his eyes and listen to the thundering of the water against the rock. The sheer might of the ocean made him feel so small, so powerless, and there was something strangely comforting in that.

They stood at the railing overlooking one of the openings in the rock, watching the light dance wild on the tempestuous waves.

"Mama," Benny said, "is it true that today is the evacuation?"

Benny sensed his mother stiffening, but she nodded.

"So Aunt Svetka —"

"Don't," she snapped and turned away.

Benny felt frustrated tears prick at his eyes. He did not understand why Mama no longer let him talk about Aunt Svetka. She and Uncle Mickey were the only family they had in Israel, and up until a year and a half ago Benny practically lived on the fishing boat belonging to his father and Uncle Mickey in Neve Adva. It was Uncle Mickey who showed Benny how to gut and clean a fish, and when they brought it home, Aunt Svetka would fry it up and serve it with her sour cream sauce. Benny could never get enough of that dish. If he closed his eyes and concentrated, he could almost smell the aroma of that bubbling pan as she set it down in front of him.

He understood that they'd had a fight when his parents decided to leave Neve Adva and move to Betzet, but he'd never actually seen any harsh words exchanged, and he found it disconcerting. One day Mama and Aunt Svetka were talking, and the next day they weren't, and whenever he tried to ask why, Mama's jaw would go hard and she would snap at him to be quiet. They didn't even say goodbye when they left Neve Adva to move to Betzet, and any time Benny tried to mention Uncle Mickey or Aunt Svetka to either of his parents, their faces went stony and they either changed the subject or didn't seem to hear him. This whole thing bewildered him. He and Kinneret fought all the time, and they had gone through short periods of refusing to speak to one another, but they always made up in the end. Is this what happens with grown-up siblings, he wondered?

Furthermore, he understood that the disengagement from Gaza meant that Aunt Svetka would be moving. And if the whole fight had been about moving, maybe they could fix it now? Where would Aunt Svetka and Uncle Mickey move? Somewhere by the sea, probably, so Uncle Mickey could still work as a fisherman. He wondered if they packed all their things onto the fishing boat and sailed up the coast. As he exited the cave, into the welcoming embrace of the light and open air and the lighter splashing sound of the waves, he scanned the shoreline for fishing boats.

As they approached the parking lot on their way back, Benny had his eye on the ice cream stand and wondered if it would be prudent to remind his mother of her promise of popsicles; but then he almost crashed into her as she halted in place. The *beep . . . beep . . . beep . . . beeeeeep* from the radio in the ice cream stand announced the commencement of the one o'clock news. Mama dug out her wallet and handed Kinneret two twenty-shekel bills.

"No more than ten shekels per kid," she said. "Get me a Cola. But only if it's cold." She nodded toward a lookout point close by. "I'll wait there." The children set off. "Watch for cars," she shouted after them.

———

"Where do you think Aunt Svetka and Uncle Mickey will move?" Benny asked Kinneret as soon as their mother was out of earshot.

Kinneret shrugged. "Ashdod, maybe? I don't know."

"Can I have a large ice cream cone?" Levana piped up, skipping next to them with her long brown ponytail bouncing.

"You'll never finish it," Kinneret said.

"I will, I will! I'm eight now! I can eat a big one!"

"I'll finish it if she doesn't," Benny offered, ever the gentleman.

"Fine." Kinneret surveyed the poster displaying the ice cream options.

"Do you think they'll make up now that they've moved?" Benny pressed.

"Who?" Kinneret asked absently.

"Mama and Aunt Svetka."

"Aunt Svetka has to be willing to talk to Mama again first. Adults are weird about stuff like this. When they fight about something it's never really about the thing."

Benny had no idea what that meant.

"So it wasn't just about moving?"

"No, you idiot. It was because Mama decided to leave Neve Adva after the government decided to evacuate it. Aunt Svetka thought she was being a traitor and a coward and that the disengagement wouldn't happen if it weren't for people like us who cooperated with the government. So even now that it's all over, she probably still thinks of Mama as a traitor."

Benny stared at the ice cream poster without really seeing anything on it. For the first time in his life, he didn't really feel hungry for ice cream.

"So..." he pressed. "Do you think Aunt Svetka will ever forgive her?"

"I don't know!" Kinneret snapped. "Stop nagging me already, you pest! Let me choose an ice cream in peace!"

Benny fell silent. The newscaster on the radio babbled on about settlers and soldiers and Kissufim Checkpoint.

———

When the children rejoined their mother, she was leaning against a large stone, looking out over the sea, taking a deep drag from a cigarette.

"Mama," Kinneret scolded, "I thought you had quit."

Mama turned and gave her a cold stare. "Where's my Cola?"

"Oh. Oops. I forgot."

"Never mind. Just give me the change." She held out her hand and Kinneret deposited the money into it. Mama examined it, counting it out, and when she had satisfied herself that the children had, indeed, spent no more than 10 shekels per kid, she slipped the change into the pocket of her shorts. She threw the half-smoked cigarette onto the ground and stamped on it. "Let's go down to the beach."

———

The rocky seashore by the northern border is not ideal for swimming. The rocks are jagged and painful to step on with bare feet. But Kinneret found a good spot for the three of them to sit and dip their feet in the waves. Benny watched his mother stroll away from them along the shoreline, and then brought his attention back to his own feet, bobbing up and down as the water bubbled and seethed against the rock he was sitting on. He stared up at the cliff rising above them, thinking of the movie at Rosh Hanikra that explained how the grottos were formed. Thousands of years of water carving away at the limestone. It was so hard to wrap his head around this paradox: the firm rock beneath him was the thing that yielded in the end, and the gentle fluid running between his toes, a substance with no form or solidity, was what prevailed in its slow, persistent power. Perhaps Aunt Svetka — soft, gentle Aunt Svetka — was like the water lapping at his feet, appearing yielding but slowly carving away at his solid, harsh mother.

Papa picked up the family from the beach on his way home from work in Nahariya. They were all exhausted and sunburned, and Levana fell asleep as soon as the car started moving. The rest of them sat in silence, staring out the windows at the orangey afternoon light filtering through the eucalyptus trees.

When they turned the corner toward their driveway, Benny was thrown forward into his seatbelt as Baruch braked suddenly, waking Levana with a jerk. Benny peeked ahead through the windshield. There was a blue Mazda parked in front of their house, and he recognized it immediately.

"Isn't that . . . ?" Kinneret whispered.

There they were: Benny could see their forms through the windshield, Aunt Svetka and Uncle Mickey hanging there in suspended animation. Mickey seemed to have stopped mid-step as he paced back and forth on the porch; Svetka was sitting on the porch swing, hugging herself and staring at the ground.

It was as though someone had pressed the pause button. Nobody moved, and nobody seemed to know what to do.

Except Benny.

He unbuckled his seatbelt and threw open the door, stumbling out of the car.

"Uncle Mickey!" He launched himself up the stairs to the porch and threw his arms around his stunned uncle, burying his face in Uncle Mickey's shirt, which smelled of salt and sweat and fish. Uncle Mickey hugged him tight, kissing him repeatedly on the top of his head. Soon Benny felt another small body slam into him from behind, and then another bigger one — his sisters had joined the embrace, and Uncle Mickey was laughing and crying at the same time. When Benny finally let go, his father's arm reached over him to shake Uncle Mickey's, and Uncle Mickey pulled him into an embrace, too.

Benny turned around, backing away from the clump of hugs and kisses to seek his mother. She was still sitting there in the front seat, staring straight ahead of her, looking as though she had forgotten how to get out of the car.

Benny walked over to her side of the car and opened the door for her. She turned her eyes on him, and they lacked their usual fierceness; in fact, Benny was astonished to see that they were wide and watery and her lip was quivering. Her expression wasn't punishing; it was imploring.

Benny hesitated, then offered a hand.

Olga stared at his hand for a few seconds, then unbuckled her seatbelt and slid her legs around, her movements slow and deliberate as though each one took a monumental amount of effort. She shifted her weight onto her feet, pushing herself out of the seat, and then straightened, taking a wobbly step forward. Benny snatched her hand and led her around the front of the car.

Svetka had already descended the stairs, still hugging herself, and now stood in front of them. Benny glanced from his mother to his aunt. They were both hunched, collapsed on themselves, eyes on the ground, pale. His mother had never looked so small to him before.

None of them said a word for a long time.

Then, finally, Svetka whispered something.

"Forgive me," she said. "Forgive me, please."

Two simple words in Russian. And as Benny watched Olga's face — a mirror image of the woman standing in front of them — he could almost see those words break through the stony barriers of her pain and let the love come rushing in like the sea bursting through the rock at Rosh Hanikra.

"Svetka," she said, and threw her arms around her sister. Benny almost sobbed with relief.

"I'm sorry," Svetka whimpered into her sister's shoulder. "I'm so sorry."

Olga pulled away, wiping the tears from her face, and took a deep breath.

"Come," she said, taking Benny's hand. "Let's start working on dinner."

THESE BONES
SHALL LIVE

Master of the Universe,
　　Do we really have to do this today?

Rabbanit Oriya told me I should write You every day, and I don't dare neglect a single instruction she has given me. I owe that woman my life; I don't know where I'd be without the guidance she gave me after Aharon was killed. I would call her, but it's two in the morning and I wouldn't want to wake her for this. Besides, I have a feeling she would tell me that the fact that I really don't want to write to You today is a sign that it's more important than ever. She's a wise and infuriating woman.

Of course it was a horrible day. I knew it would be. But You know me; I've made an art of glossing those over, especially when I'm in the public eye. I expected it to be hard just like I expected the day of the expulsion to be hard. I'd had months to mentally prepare myself, and I did everything in my power to make it as pleasant and gentle as possible for the children: to show them the strong, cheerful Talia, the one who accepts Your cruel decrees with love and faith and resonates with the belief that everything is truly for the best even if we can't see how. And when the army came to evacuate us, I played the part to a T. I think even that soldier who fell apart on my couch was sufficiently fooled. Many people are. I've become an expert at it in the years since Aharon was killed. That's the role You gave me by taking him, after all, isn't it? I'm a symbol. An embodiment of the strength of the Jewish people, of the settler movement, of the religious Zionist movement, a symbol of everything we stand for. People look to you for strength and inspiration when you become an IDF or terror widow. Holding it together is my primary job in life right now.

Well, to hell with that.

I hate You today.

I hate You so much.

There, I said it.

Re-interment: such an odd idea. It's sort of like the false sense of security I felt when Aharon survived that first terror attack. You figure lightning won't strike twice. There's no way he'll get hurt again. What are the chances? And then, of all people... You had to take him. Like an exceptionally cruel joke — the same person, in the same greenhouse! So you lay your loved one to rest; you give his body back to the earth, bury it, engrave his name in stone. That's the idea of burial — eternity, finality. The finality of it is part of what helps you process. You understand that he's gone, you really understand, you feel it in your bones, and that's how you start to work through it. It's hell, but it's a hell set in stone, it's a path many others have walked before you and you just set one foot in front of another. And maybe they're the worst two years of your life, worse than anything you could have imagined, but you survive, you drag yourself up from the deepest depths of despair, and you know nothing will ever be the same but you start to adjust to this new reality and you start to feel like you're finding your footing.

And then the government comes along and tells you that everything you've built and everything you know and love is going to disappear now, reduced to rubble, and you have to pack up your things and decide what you're going to take and what you're going to leave. And those bones, those bones that are supposed to be buried there for eternity, they tell you that you have to take them with you. And the eternity that tells you where you're supposed to be on this horrible journey, the only lighthouse in this black sea of bereavement, suddenly it's extinguished and you don't know where you are anymore, the beginning becomes the end and the end becomes the beginning and you're back to the shiva but only for a day and it's been two years but what does time even mean anymore? You have to have another funeral. You have to rend your clothes again. Can I use the same shirt I used the first time? Do I sew up the old tear and re-rip it, or can I just rip the existing tear twice as deep, right down to the heart? Can I rip it apart completely? Can I burn the bloody thing and throw the ashes into the sea so I can't possibly ever do this again?

And then like in Ezekiel's prophecy the dry bones rise from the ground, only they don't grow skin and sinews, and You don't breathe the breath of life into them; they are merely lowered back into a different grave somewhere else and the whole exile starts all over again and everybody is mourning, but we're mourning so much more than a death, we've all just lost everything, but also we're still here in the Land of Israel, living the dream, but burying the dream, but…just…this is not how the prophecy ends and none of this makes any sense.

They made us wait at Kissufim Checkpoint for the hearses to come. Most of the others went to Jerusalem for the main ceremony. There's a part of me that still regrets choosing to have Aharon reburied in Safed instead of joining the others from the Gush Katif cemetery. But it's probably for the best. I don't think I would have been able to stand the massive crowd on the Mount of Olives, and I don't think it would have been good for the children either. And since Aharon was the only one from Neve Adva who died there, at least some of our neighbors would be with us. Still, there was something lonely about parting with the evacuees from the rest of the Gush and going our own way, and the drive…such a long drive. The kids spent the entire ride bickering and crying and yelling and I swear I was this close to pulling over right there in the middle of the highway and throwing them all to the four winds — especially Nehorai, who just *would not stop whining.* When we got to Safed I finally realized that he had a fever, and I felt like the worst mother on the face of the earth that I had been so impatient with him the whole drive. Of course I hadn't thought to bring Acamoli. I'm lucky I remembered to bring my own head. I didn't know what to do — should he miss the funeral? He was too little to remember the first one; wouldn't this one give him a little more closure? But how could I let him stand out there in the heat with a fever?

An endless march of double-edged-sword situations, that's what parenting is, and it was hard even when there were two of us.

I hate You.

But Your people are amazing. The first person I saw after feeling Nehorai's forehead was Shulamit. I stuttered something to her about Acamoli, remembering that she's a nurse — as if that's supposed to help, as if she walks around with a hospital pharmacy in her pocket. We were standing there in the cemetery parking lot, not a Superpharm in sight, but somehow within ten minutes someone handed me a bottle, only You could know where from. So after dosing him up and satisfying myself that he was drinking I decided to let him stay for the funeral.

It seemed that everybody from Neve Adva was there — even Olga and Svetka, hand in hand, would you believe it? There was even a young woman who walked up to me and started to introduce herself before I found myself grabbing her arm — "You're Tali!" I exclaimed. "The soldier who helped us leave!" She nodded, and I gave her a big hug. I was so touched that she came, God. It really warmed my heart.

And I needed that.

I felt physically ill when they removed the coffin from the hearse. It felt like a scene straight from all those nightmares I'd been having about Aharon bursting out of the coffin with rotting flesh hanging from his bones and screaming out to me. I knew I should never have Googled how long it takes a corpse to decompose. They wouldn't even let me see his body after he was killed. I kept trying to force myself to imagine him only as I remembered him, with his wild red beard and slightly crooked smile, but the images came and haunted me at night, especially after I read the forensic reports. Still do sometimes. The mortar shell hit him right in the chest and I had so many nightmares about watching him being blown apart by it.

Just one of the many things I never told that woman who interviewed me for L'Isha Magazine. Remember that? She brought a photographer who spent twenty minutes trying to make me laugh, and the big bold headline they put next to my photo was *Still Smiling*. I never read the article. People told me it was deeply inspiring. I threw my copy of the magazine straight in the trash when it came in the mail.

Anyway.

Of course it was a horrible day. But I really started to question Your benevolence when Nehorai passed out during *E-l Maleh Rachamim*. I didn't even notice. It was Emuna who caught him and got my attention.

Of all the...

I hate You.

My mom told me I should stay at the funeral and let her take Nehorai instead of me, but the thought of my son being there without me was more horrifying than the idea of missing the rest of the ceremony. And of course through the entire ambulance ride I cursed myself thoroughly for not sending him back to my parents' house with Ima before it began. A double-edged-sword decision, and I definitely made the wrong choice, and I hated myself for it and I hated You for giving it to me in the first place. Why do You torture me like this?

The doctors at Ziv Hospital were sweet and respectful and Nehorai perked right up after they started the IV. I sat there with my usual fake smile plastered on my face until that nurse turned up to check his blood pressure.

She was my age or a little younger, on the stocky side, from Ukraine, I think, or Latvia; a former Soviet for sure. Her movements were quick and precise. She gave me a scrutinizing look as she removed the cuff from Nehorai's arm.

"Aren't you Talia Cohen?"

I groaned inwardly, but kept my plastic smile on and nodded.

"You missed the end of your husband's second funeral?"

I nodded again.

She glanced around briefly. "Why is nobody else here to be with you and your son?"

I shrugged. "My parents are caring for my other children. Someone had to."

"Someone had to..." she echoed, examining Nehorai's chart and jotting down the results of her exam. Then she looked up and gave me a piercing look with her icy blue eyes. "I saw that article about you in L'Isha," she said. "To tell you the truth, it made me feel awful."

That was not the sort of comment I was used to.

"I lost my husband in a car accident just around the time you lost yours," she said. "Not much glory in that death. There were no reporters chasing after me, and thank God for that. I was a wreck. I thought my life would be over. I couldn't get out of bed for two months. My kids went to live with my sister. My whole life fell apart. It's still in pieces. At least I'm back at work now, but the kids are only with me part of the time. And there you were, smiling on that magazine cover, and I just...I hated you. I hated you for being able to be so positive and move on with your life and be all full of faith when I was such a basket case. I felt like such a coward, such a weakling, so hopeless."

Well, obviously, by that point I had dropped the smile, and started to cry. She stood there frowning at me. Nehorai was staring at both of us in shock, and I felt terrible that he had to listen to this, and so, so angry at this woman for daring to say those things in front of him.

"Do you really think I never fell apart?" I demanded. "Do you really think I never felt despair?"

"Then why didn't you show it?" she asked, and her voice cracked, and I saw a tear leak out of the corner of her eye. "I didn't need to see you being strong. Everyone told me to be strong. I needed to see you falling apart. I needed to see that it was okay to fall apart."

"I owe you nothing."

"Yes, you owe nothing to any of us, but you act like you do. You think putting on that smile and pretending to be strong helps the rest of us be strong, but it's not true. It's not. Being strong doesn't mean you never break." And with that she swept out of the room.

How dare she?

How *dare* she?!

I wanted to report her to the head of the department, to the social worker, to somebody, anybody. But I never got her name, and she didn't turn up again during the whole shift, and by the time the doctor came with the release form all I wanted to do was get out of there and collapse in bed. Not that I was able to sleep once I got home, of course, which is why I'm here writing to You at two in the morning.

Not that I've slept much in the past few months anyway.

I have to say, though, sitting here and writing this out, after having a chance to calm down and get some distance...I'm starting to wonder if there's a reason You sent her to me.

Maybe she's right.

Maybe the Nation of Israel doesn't need me to be a symbol of anything.

Maybe it's not my responsibility to hold it together.

Maybe I should just let You scatter me like so many dry bones in the Valley of the Shadow of Death, and let You decide when and how and whether to pull me back together.

Maybe I should be allowed to grieve and to be angry and to fall apart whenever and however I have to, and leave that whole resurrection business to You.

Wow. I am overcome with exhaustion all of a sudden, weary right down to my bones. I should try to get some rest if I can. Tomorrow is going to be a hard day.

Just like every day.

I hate You.

I love You.

I love Aharon.

I miss him so much.

I hate You for taking him from me and for making me bury him again.

I hate You for letting them uproot every earthbound trace of the home we built together.

I miss things being simple between You and me.

God, am I tired.

Talia

Neighbors

Summer 2005

Dear Edna,

You will not believe who just moved into the house next door.

There are five brats. Two of whom are adults. I recognized the woman from television — did you watch the news during the disengagement a few weeks back? All those settlers screaming at the poor soldiers who were just standing there trying to do their jobs? So I'm pretty sure she's one of them. Horrible. She was wearing the same stupid orange scarf. Heavily pregnant, too. They'd better not spawn many more little terrors while they're here. I've already made peace with the fact that my tulips in the front yard are history, but if they make much more noise than they already do I'll have to install a soundproof wall to get any rest around here.

I'm worried that there are more families like them on the way. There are a few religious families in Bat Hefer, but, you know, they're the normal, sane kind, where both parents work normal jobs and the wife wears a hat with her hair showing, and they space their kids apart two years or more. These new neighbors, God help me. Their youngest can't be much older than a year old, and I tell you, that woman is due to pop any day now. I think the oldest is still in kindergarten, too. Can you imagine? She'll have four kids five and under? At least one of them is crying at any given moment. I haven't dared to peek inside but I am absolutely certain the floor is covered in Cheerios and the walls are smeared with Bamba and all manner of filth.

In short, I've put social services on speed dial. At least the noise distracts me a little from my backache.

Love,

Hedva

Dear Edna,

Yes, the back is doing a little better, and the doctor said there's no reason it should still be hurting me, but you know doctors, they never believe anything I say.

Yuval? I wish I could tell you how he is. Last time he called was three weeks and four days ago. I tell you, everything would have been different with Pini. He would have called me every day, even if he'd been busy like Yuval always is. He would never have neglected his mother like Yuval does. If there is a God, He is cruel for taking away the son that would have taken care of me in my old age.

Oh, and the situation with the neighbors — it's only getting worse. Yesterday, the mother came around the neighborhood handing out cookies and introducing herself, "Hi, I'm Naama, I was just expelled from Gush Katif." As if none of us had figured that out. She looked like she was ready to give a whole speech, but

I snapped at her that I have diabetes and to tell her kids to stay away from my tulips.

Love,

Hedva

Dear Edna,

I know you mean well, Edna, but I just hate when people say that — that God only takes the best of them. What did God need Pini for? Does God have diabetes and arthritis too? Aren't there enough wonderful young men up there to keep Him company by now?

You wouldn't believe the nerve of this settler woman, Edna. She's been passing out flyers advertising an evening of solidarity with evacuees of Gush Katif, where she will be speaking about the "expulsion" as they call it. She came by and tried to hand me one, and when I told her I wasn't interested, she asked me if I'd like to come have a cup of tea at their house. I told her I couldn't; I don't remember what excuse I made up, and when she asked if she could come have one at *my* house sometime, I was too shocked to say no. She said she'd come by tomorrow in the morning. She has no idea what she's getting herself into, Edna.

Love,

Hedva

Dear Edna,

I don't know if my last letter reached you yet, but I just have to tell you about my conversation with that new neighbor woman.

She came at around nine, presumably after dropping off all the brats at their preschools. You know me, I'm not going to receive any guest without some hospitality, so I brought the tea in the fine china and everything. It's been a while since I've used that set. Do you remember it? The one my mother, of blessed memory, brought from her heritage trip to Ukraine, with the blue floral designs. I'm pretty sure I used it the first few times you came over for tea. I stopped getting it out when Yigal started throwing dishes. He may have broken my arm that one time, but if he'd broken my mother's china, I tell you, that would have been the end of him. Anyway, it was nice to get it down from the top cabinet, even it if it did make my back worse for a while. I even noticed that the package of cookies I've been keeping around for guests said "kosher" on the label.

As expected, after a few minutes of small talk she started yammering to me about her life in Gaza. She rattled on and on about how much they had sacrificed to live there, and how they'd been treated like second-class citizens with unreliable electricity and far away from the nearest commodities, living on the front lines to protect us all from the Palestinians, blah blah blah. The self-righteousness was sickening.

And then, Edna, get this — she told me the name of the settlement where she lived.

Neve Adva.

The same Neve Adva where Pini was stabbed trying to protect a settler.

"You don't know anything about sacrifice," I told her. "My son died protecting you and the rest of your little settler friends down there in Neve Adva." Oh, the look on her face, Edna, it was priceless. I told her in great detail how Pini didn't even want to serve in Gaza and none of us had chosen that fate for him, and how it was all for nothing, and about all the hopes and dreams that he had that went up in smoke because someone had to protect her and her little brats living in the middle of nowhere. She was talking to me about sacrifices? Does she have any idea what it feels like to wake in the middle of the night and just know, *know* that your favorite son is gone, and to lie there awake, afraid to move to confirm your prediction, until the knock comes at the door, and then to open the door and see them standing there, the casualty officers with the grim look on their faces, to be engulfed in black forever? I started to cry, because, well, you know me, I can't talk about Pini without crying, and she started to cry too, and when I was done talking she just sat there staring at the floor for a long time.

I have no idea how it had never occurred to her that other people had made sacrifices for her to be there, too. Did she think none of us pay taxes? That it didn't cost millions to maintain a military presence in Gaza? That it didn't cost lives — not only of settlers, but of soldiers, little boys who never volunteered to be out there like she did? It's not that I'm against settlement entirely, you know, if not for pioneers we wouldn't have a country, and I know that. My own parents came from Eastern Europe after one too many pogroms and helped put up the tower of Tel Tzur during the "wall and tower" operation. It's not like they would have had any place to go home to. It's just that you have to know when to cut your losses, Edna. Gaza is a tiny, godforsaken little strip of beach filled with nothing but sand and terrorists. We don't need it, you know? We've got a whole big empty Negev to fill if you want to be all brave and pioneering.

So I said all this while she sat there silently. I don't know how much she heard or understood, but after a while she got up and thanked me and left without another word.

Who knows. Maybe I got through to her. Maybe they can be taught after all. Next I should tell her why she needs to stop having so many kids.

Love,

Hedva

Dear Edna,

Wouldn't you know, yesterday there was a knock on my door and all three of the little neighbor kids were standing there with a box of sugar-free cookies for me. They were the good kind, too. (The cookies. Not the kids.)

Yuval finally came to visit yesterday, too. His kids sit and watch TV all day like lumps. Those neighbor kids, they may be feral wild animals, but at least they know how to play outside like we used to when we were kids. Remember how our kids used to build forts in the grassy area at the end of our street? Those were the days. I'll never have a neighbor as great as you and your family were to us, Edna. I'll never forget how you supported me through the divorce.

I hope your husband feels better soon.

Love,

Hedva

———

Dear Edna,

You know, I usually do love that show, and yes, I saw the special episode about the disengagement. I don't know, Edna, I may have found it hilarious a month or two ago, but something about it bothered me this time. These settlers, they're crazy, and stupid, and they deserve some of the ridicule, but it was over-the-top. This Naama, I have to admit, she's really not all that bad. She's been dropping in every day to ask if I need something, even brought her oldest kid to help her wash my floor once, and she sometimes stays to chat a bit.

I'm so glad to hear Shimon is doing better! Let me know if you'd like me to look at any more of his bloodwork before that lazy excuse for a doctor gets back to you.

Love,

Hedva

———

Dear Edna,

Boy, do I have a story for you!

Remember how I mentioned that Naama — you know, the settler neighbor — was pregnant? In the past few weeks we've been chatting a lot, as I mentioned, and I told her about how I used to work as a midwife at Tel Hashomer. So on Wednesday morning I was watching television and there was a sharp knock on the door. I went to answer it and there she was, white as my bathroom tiles, dripping amniotic fluid everywhere. Her water had broken suddenly and she was having intense contractions every few minutes and there was no one else home, so she had just called the ambulance but she was afraid they wouldn't make it in time. I didn't think twice; I walked her over to the couch and went to fetch some towels. I don't think I've moved that quickly since I retired, Edna! I didn't realize how much I've missed my work. Sure enough, I heard that low grunting sound women make when they're pushing, and I rushed to her side and lay the towels underneath her and helped her remove her underwear. The baby came very smoothly and easily — fourth birth, no surprise there — and he was already all cleaned up and ready for the hospital by the time the medics arrived. A beautiful, plump little boy. I estimated him to be around 3.9 kg, and I was only 100 grams off — 3.8. Naama kept kissing my cheeks, and I haven't felt so pleased with myself since I got that award for excellence at the gala at Tel Hashomer, I tell you. I almost offered to go with her, but that seemed silly, since her husband was on his way and so was her mother. So I satisfied myself by cleaning up the mess. The house felt awfully quiet and lonely afterward. Who would have imagined I'd miss the sound of a newborn baby crying? I'm getting sentimental in my old age!

The *brit milah* is next Wednesday. Do you think I should get out my old knitting needles and make him a blanket? It's been so long, I'm not sure I remember how!

Love,

Hedva

Dear Edna,

Yes, I did go to the *brit* in the end, and I did make them a blanket — it came out a little lumpy, but I don't think they'll mind. In any case, it was nothing compared to what they gave me at that *brit*, Edna. You'll never believe what they named the baby. Pinchas. Pini. Yes, after my Pini. I haven't cried so hard in years. He has the sweetest little cheeks, Edna. You've never seen such pinchable cheeks in your life.

Love,

Hedva

REFUGEES

August 18, 2006 | Ehud Hazan

Last week, while most of my colleagues were dodging Katyushas in Haifa and Kiryat Shmona, I was driving in the opposite direction—and not to get away from the rockets. I went to Kibbutz Karmia in the western Negev. Specifically, to the caravilla village that houses around fifty families evacuated from Gush Katif exactly a year ago.

I know what you're thinking: the disengagement, Hazan? Really? The entire north of our country is pockmarked with Katyusha craters and you want to talk to us about whiny settlers waxing nostalgic about their lost beach houses?

Yes, I do.

The caravilla village at Kibbutz Karmia looks like a grid of identical dollhouses arranged in neat rows in a playground sandbox. The caravillas, so-called luxury mobile homes, look pleasant enough on the outside; cheerfully painted pinkish brown, with triangular terra-cotta tiled roofs, they look like something out of a child's drawing.

I first met Rabbi Shlomo two years ago in the middle of Kissufim Highway: my car broke down on my way to an interview, and he pulled over to help. I spent the afternoon in his home in Neve Adva, a tiny settlement near Neve Dekalim.

I wouldn't have admitted it then, but his kindness, and the tight-knit spirit of the community he was part of, stuck with me.

Even so, it turns out I knew very little about him.

For example, I hadn't even noticed that he is missing his right leg from the knee down.

He was sitting on the cramped patio in the sweltering heat as I drove up, his prosthetic resting against the wall of the caravilla, and his thigh propped up on a chair. He was dabbing at the stump with a towel. Being the tactful gentleman that I am, the first words out of my mouth were, "What happened to your leg?"

He looked up and eyed me wearily.

"I don't know," he said, "but if you're up in Lebanon reporting on this war, send it my regards."

He pulled his pant leg over the stump and gestured toward a plastic chair.

"This is from the First Lebanon War?" I ascended the wooden steps and took a seat. "How is it that I didn't notice?"

He shrugged. "Many people didn't. I functioned pretty well in Neve Adva. Shulamit?"

The screen door swung open, and Rabbi Shlomo's wife appeared. The circles under her eyes were darker and the lines in her forehead harsher than I had remembered. She nodded at me without smiling and retreated back into the house, then emerged a minute later with two cups of ice water.

"I'd invite you to sit inside," said Rabbi Shlomo, "but our air conditioner is broken and we haven't been able to dredge up the funds to get it fixed."

He stared at the glass in his hand, swirling the ice cubes in a slow circle.

"I read your column," he said finally. "The one about the evacuation."

I waited.

"It was...interesting," he went on. "Not your usual fare."

"I'll take that as a compliment."

"You should."

Another pause.

"So..." I glanced at the surrounding dollhouses. "How have you been?"

As a disabled war veteran, Rabbi Shlomo has been unable to work since his injury and receives a stipend from the government. It's not much of an income. His health declined significantly after the disengagement, especially while living in a hotel room in Ashkelon in the three months before they were relocated to the caravilla. His wife Shulamit has had to reduce her hours working as a nurse at Soroka to care for him.

Money is tight, and morale is low.

"We're refugees," Rabbi Shlomo summarized. "Refugees in our own land."

"That sounds familiar," I said quietly. Rabbi Shlomo probably didn't catch that I was referring not to former settlers, but to Palestinians; I decided not to press the point, and to ask him about his kids instead. He had three adult daughters who were married and living elsewhere when we first met, but I remembered his youngest son calling me a Nazi the night before the evacuation. That son is in the army now—"Not in Lebanon, I hope?" I cut in. He answered, with visible relief, that his son was in the tech corps.

"At least we have our community here," he went on. "But the situation is unsustainable. Lots of people here were farmers. They can't find work. They just sit around drinking coffee and feeling useless. My wife..." Rabbi Shlomo glanced toward the door, then leaned in and lowered his voice. "She drives back to Kissufim almost every day."

"What, to try to get in?"

"No, of course not. Just to see it. She stands there and cries."

He leaned back, watching my reaction.

"And these shoeboxes..." He waved a hand at the caravilla behind him. "They're better than a caravan, I'll give you that, but they don't keep out the heat or the cold, and most importantly, they don't keep out the rockets."

He asked me if I'd heard about the rocket that hit one of the caravillas nearby in February, badly injuring a baby. I had not. "It's a miracle no one died," he said.

I asked to see the interior of the caravilla, despite the lack of air conditioning. Shulamit gave me the full—and extremely short—tour. The place was sixty square meters: two bedrooms, one bathroom, a tiny kitchen, a modest living-slash-dining room with a small plastic table and a little Ikea couch. I recognized the oriental rug at its feet, but nothing else.

"We sold most of our furniture," Shulamit said. "Nothing would fit, and we can't afford to keep it in storage indefinitely."

When we had rejoined Rabbi Shlomo on the patio, the two sank into a melancholy silence.

"May I ask you a tough question?" I finally asked.

They exchanged a tense glance. I took their silence as a yes.

"What would you say to those who would argue that you brought this upon yourselves?"

"Upon ourselves?"

"In moving to Gush Katif in the first place. In not leaving earlier, or cooperating better with the government."

"We moved to Gush Katif because we believed it was the right thing to do," Rabbi Shlomo said, an edge in his voice. "For ourselves, and for our country and for our people. The fact that we were thrown out of our homes to the four winds doesn't make that less true. On the contrary."

"It's been a year," Shulamit cut in. "We have still not seen a shekel of the compensation we were promised. And we were among the first to file for it after the expulsion. There are those who didn't file at all, and I understand them. The government has betrayed us at every turn. You think we should have trusted them?"

———————————

I decided to stop at Kissufim Checkpoint before heading home.

A stone has been erected there that reads: "Here, in the Gaza Strip, the citizens of Gush Katif and the soldiers of the IDF lived and fought side by side for four decades."

If I'd had a permanent marker on me, I might have been arrested later for defacing a public monument by tacking on "at the expense of millions of innocent Palestinians, who are still not free from their tyranny."

I looked beyond the fence at the road stretching out toward the horizon. I thought of Shulamit weeping there; but I also thought of that Palestinian woman I had met at that spot the night before the disengagement, fighting to be allowed into Israel to receive life-saving cancer treatment. I thought about the serene beach of Neve Adva, where I had washed my face the morning of the evacuation, and imagined that woman's children playing in the waves. I thought about Moshe Skolnik's greenhouses, and about the peppers and cherry tomatoes that the poor people of Gaza might now be able to grow.

If Rabbi Shlomo feels like a refugee in his own land, he now has a tiny taste of how his former neighbors, the people of Gaza, have felt since 1948. His life may be hard now, but theirs are infinitely harder.

That doesn't mean I don't sympathize with his loss.

That doesn't mean I don't think he deserves better.

We can believe that the settlement movement was immoral and the disengagement necessary, and still acknowledge that we made a painful sacrifice for the good of our country.

We can only hope that time will prove — in another year, another two years, another eight years — that those sacrifices were worth it.

SHELTER

Summer 2014

The swell of the air raid siren caught Maayan off-guard, even though she'd been expecting one the entire drive to Tel Aviv. Her hands clenched around the steering wheel, jerking the car a little as she swerved over two lanes of traffic on Yitzchak Sadeh. She pulled over at the side of the road, fumbled frantically with her seat belt, and shoved the door open. As she got out of the car, she scanned the street, trying to spot a flow of people that would indicate the location of a bomb shelter.

"Over here!"

Maayan registered a young man in a tank top and shorts standing at the entrance to one of the nearby buildings, waving his arms over his head. She slammed the door shut and sprinted toward him. He gave her a crooked smile as he pointed her down a spiral staircase leading below the building.

"What's the rush?" he asked. "We've got a whole ninety seconds."

Maayan ignored his comment and ran down the stairs, almost tripping over the hem of her skirt. She heard the man's footsteps pounding behind her. The steel door was open, but the shelter was pitch black inside. She groped for the lights. Her heart was pounding so strong, she could hear her blood pumping in her ears.

"Here." His arm brushed against Maayan's shoulder as he reached across her to turn a knob. The lights came on to reveal a small, grungy room that looked like it had been painted white ten years ago. The air inside was stale and musty. A few broken skeletons of chairs were scattered at the other end of the shelter.

The man leaned against the wall, digging into a box of cigarettes. He paused when his eyes met Maayan's.

"Want one?" he offered, jerking the box upward.

She shook her head and tsked no.

"Do you mind?" He pulled out a cigarette and stuck it between his lips.

She did, but was too shy — and pumped full of adrenaline — to protest.

He didn't seem all that interested in an answer, anyway. He pulled a lighter out of his pocket and held it up to the cigarette.

BOOM. The ground quivered, rattling the door on its hinges, and a gasp escaped from Maayan's lips. "*Shema Yisrael.*"

"That one was Iron Dome," said the man, muffled by the now-lit cigarette. He tucked the box and the lighter into his pocket and closed his eyes, taking a long drag. "They're louder when they're intercepted."

Another boom rocked the building. Maayan had heard her share of exploding rockets, but she hadn't known that about Iron Dome. Now that she thought about it, of course it made sense; a missile hitting another missile would make a bigger explosion than a missile hitting the ground. She liked to visualize the Iron Dome defense system as the hand of God Himself picking rockets out of the sky to protect His chosen people from harm. It hadn't occurred to her to visualize it as a pair of bombs meeting in mid-air, though she knew, in theory, that that was how it worked.

She started reciting Psalm 23 by heart.

"So what are you doing in Tel Aviv?" the man asked.

Maayan raised her hand with her fingertips touching and palm facing up — the Israeli gesture for "just a minute" — as she finished reciting the psalm. When she finished, she cast an appraising look at the man. He seemed around her age, and he was handsome, in a rugged Tel Aviv way: the browned, muscular shoulders bulging from the tank top, the hairy legs covered only marginally by the shorts, the flip-flops, the mussed up I-don't-care hairstyle, the five o'clock shadow.

"What makes you think I don't live here?" she asked finally.

He laughed heartily. "You?" He scanned her up and down, and the hairs on the back of her neck prickled with the uncomfortable, irrational sensation that he could see right through her clothes. "Sleeves to the elbow in the middle of August, floor-sweeping skirt? You're a settler. I can smell it on you."

Maayan set her jaw, not bothering to hide her irritation. She had put up with plenty of sneering remarks about her gender and religious affiliation in her day, but this was a new level. "Oh?" she said. "How do settlers *smell*?"

"I'm right, aren't I?"

"No," Maayan said forcefully. Then she faltered. "Well…technically. I *was* a settler. Until nine years ago."

The man flicked some ash onto the floor and stamped on it with his foot.

"Nine years, huh?" he said. "Me too."

Maayan shuffled back a step in surprise. The man lifted his eyes to meet hers, and this time she held their gaze.

"Gush Katif?" she asked.

"Neve Adva."

"You're kidding! I lived one settlement over. Shoshanim."

He broke eye contact and took another puff of the cigarette, looking, for the first time, at a loss for words.

Maayan listened carefully, noticing that the siren had stopped wailing.

"It's stopped," she said.

"We're supposed to stay in here ten minutes. Falling debris. It's no joke. A hunk of missile casing landed on my friend's car the other day. Crushed the roof like a rock dropped on a birthday cake."

As Maayan contemplated the odd imagery of this simile, the siren started up again.

"And then there's that." He gave a dry chuckle.

"So you lived in Neve Adva?" Maayan studied his face more closely in the dim, yellowish light. It was hard to imagine him as a settler. "What's your name?"

"Yossi," he said. "Yossi Toledano."

"*Toledano?* You're the rabbi's son?"

He flicked some ash from his cigarette again and shrugged. Another boom shook the ground.

"How did you end up here?" Maayan asked.

He gave her a scrutinizing look. "I asked first."

Boom.

"Asked what?"

"What you're doing in Tel Aviv."

Maayan chewed on the inside of her lip, then decided to answer. "Interview."

"Job interview?"

"No." Maayan flushed a little. "Television."

Boom boom.

"What are you, a celebrity?"

Maayan laughed. "Thank God, no." She cleared her throat. "I ... I just released a book of poetry."

"Aha. 'The Poet of Shoshanim.'"

"Be'er Sheva now."

"And your name is?"

"Maayan Tzurim."

"Maayan Tzurim," he repeated, and then took another puff from the cigarette, staring into the distance. "Maayan Tzurim…" Then his eyes snapped onto her face. "Maayan Tzurim! 'Where, then, do sky and water meet? Where does one become the other?'"

Maayan gawked at him. "Where —"

"My roommate is an artsy film major. He cut that out from a magazine or something and put it on our fridge. It's been staring at me every day for months while he yells at me to put away the milk."

Maayan was completely speechless. She had never had her own poetry recited back to her by a stranger.

"It's good," he said, eyeing her briefly and lowering his eyes. "The poem."

"I'm… glad you like it," she said weakly.

"What are your other poems about?"

"I just answered several of your questions," Maayan pointed out, recovering. "Now you should answer mine."

"And what does the Poet of Be'er Sheva want to know?"

"Where were you during the expulsion?"

He took what remained of the cigarette out of his mouth and examined it closely. "'When the wine-red sun sank into the sea and scattered rays in a thousand shades….' On the roof of the synagogue. With the other kids." He tossed the cigarette butt on the ground and stamped on it.

"You were religious then, I take it."

He gave her a cold look. "And where were you, Maayan Tzurim? In the synagogue? Praying for a miracle? Praying for the Messiah to come, along with all the rest of us? Were you also suckered into the lie, the delusion, that God cares one tiny bit about what we want? That He promised us every inch of this land? Were you also told that if we only prayed hard enough, the whole thing would be turned around and we would continue living there forever?" He paused, studying Maayan's face. "Shit. I made you cry."

Maayan wiped furiously at her eyes, trying to push the images his words had so accurately conjured from her mind: the barricaded synagogue, the voices raised in desperate prayer, her eyes closed as she practically screamed Psalm 102: *Tefilla l'ani ki ya'atof*…and the sudden sensation of sturdy arms taking hold of her, lifting her, her feet losing contact with the ground of the synagogue — never to touch it again.

Another explosion rattled the room.

"I'll take that as a yes," said Yossi, stuffing his hands into his pockets. "So to answer the question you've been trying to ask, that entire experience broke me. Broke everything. I was seventeen. Threw my kippa out the window from the bus. Refused to go back to school. My dad was so furious, he wouldn't talk to me for weeks. Did you get stuck in a hotel for three months too?"

"Three?" Maayan gave a derisive laugh. "Six."

"Yeah. So because there were only three of us, I was in the room with my parents, and had to deal with them in very close quarters until we finally moved to a crummy caravilla in the middle of nowhere. My dad's a disabled army veteran and my mom wasn't able to keep her job at Soroka, so they had to dig into our compensation funds to keep buying groceries, and by the time our permanent housing was approved there was no money left. Familiar story, I assume."

Maayan nodded, thinking of the months her own dad — who had been a farmer — spent on the front porch of their caravilla, staring into space.

"I didn't want to serve in the army, but it was the only way to get away from my parents," Yossi went on. "That's where I discovered my talent for coding. So when I got out of the army, I found a job in hi-tech and moved here."

He looked up again.

"Your turn," he said.

Maayan cleared her throat, trying to regain composure. "What do you want to know?"

"Why aren't you wearing a headscarf?"

She raised an eyebrow. "I'm single."

"Single and how old?"

Maayan allowed herself a humorless laugh. "What are you, my aunt?"

"I'm guessing you aren't eighteen."

"You should never tell a girl that."

"A girl who can't handle the truth has no business being anywhere near me."

"I'm twenty-four."

"That's old to be single in your community."

"You got a *shidduch* for me?"

One corner of his mouth lifted into an amused smile, and she blushed and bit the inside of her lip. This was not the direction she had intended for this conversation to take. Cute though he might be, he was secular, and a far cry from what she would consider marriage — and therefore dating — material. She tried to rewind the conversation in her head and figure out how she had stumbled so close to flirting.

"What are the poems about?" he asked.

Maayan took a few moments to fumble for an answer.

"Lots of things." She noticed that she had been cracking her knuckles — a nervous habit — and quickly pulled her hands apart. "God. Love. Grief. The human condition. They're poems."

"You teach literature or something?"

"I study it. At Ben-Gurion University."

"Impressive that you're already published then, isn't it?"

"My professor thought the poems were ready." Her face was still warm. "But it's my turn now." She crossed her arms. "Is there anything about the religious life that you miss?"

He pursed his lips and took a few moments to answer. "If you'd asked me a year ago, I'd have said no. If you're asking me now...yes. I miss the sense of community. It was very strong in the Gush. I miss the feeling of belonging, of fitting in. I can't fit in anywhere now. It's lonely."

Maayan let that hang in the air for a few moments.

"Well, not entirely," Yossi said quickly. "There are organizations, you know, for ex-religious youth. There was this couple they paired me with, both *datlashim*, and it turned out that the guy was involved in the evacuation of Neve Adva as a soldier. What are the chances?"

"Probably similar to the chances of your ending up in a bomb shelter with a girl from Shoshanim."

"They had me over for dinner a few times. But we fell out of touch."

Maayan waited, and when he didn't go on, she said, "I imagine it's hard to stay in touch without a regular framework."

"Yeah."

They were quiet for another few moments, and then Yossi spoke again.

"There's also..." He slid down the wall and sat on the floor with his elbows on his knees. "I miss that sense of...I just had this unquestioning faith that there was justice in the universe, that God protects and defends the righteous, that the Full Redemption was just a heartbeat away. Everything was easier when I lived that way. But it was a house of cards, and the expulsion blew it over." He looked up at Maayan. "Do you still believe in God?"

"What a question. Of course I do."

"How? How do you believe in a God who both gave us the Torah and the Land of Israel, and then tore it away from us like that? How do you believe in a God who completely ignored our prayers?"

Maayan shook her head. "The God I believe in isn't a soda machine. You don't put in your five-shekel prayer and expect Him to give you a cola. That's not how it works."

He shrugged. "If God exists, then I hate Him. He just tortured us for no reason." He cast a scathing look upward. "And look what we got for our trouble. Those rockets were probably fired from my old house."

"I get mad at Him too sometimes," said Maayan. "Because I don't always know the reason. But I still believe that there always is a reason."

"Why?" The Tel Aviv irony was completely gone from his voice now. His eyes were boring into hers, almost pleading, and she felt a shiver go down her spine.

"I don't know," she said. "I just know . . . that my life is better that way."

"Doesn't it kill you that your entire life is based on something you can't prove?"

"No, because that's true for everyone, whether or not we're willing to admit it."

"What do you mean?"

"Certainty is an illusion. It's arrogance. There is very little that can be really proven without a doubt if you drill down to the fundamentals. So either you can sulk about how nothing is certain and live in nihilistic cynicism, or you can embrace mystery and live with hope."

He gave a sardonic grin. "I'm getting the sense that you're criticizing the secular worldview, Poet."

"I'm getting the sense that you were asking me to, Rabbi's Son."

Yossi didn't answer. Maayan finally noticed that the siren was no longer blaring.

"When did the siren stop?" she asked.

"I don't know. You're wondering when you can get away from me?"

"I'm wondering if I'm going to make it to my interview."

He examined his watch. "What time is your interview?"

"I'm supposed to be there at 11:30."

"You have ten minutes."

"I should go."

They studied each other.

"Want to swing by again afterward?" he said.

She took a step back, closing her fists. Did he mean that the way she thought he did?

"Perhaps," he added, casting a look around the dilapidated room, "at a more respectable venue."

It seemed that he did. Maayan knew she should probably just laugh this off, but her knees felt inexplicably rubbery.

"Are you…" she ventured, "asking me out?"

He rolled his eyes, picking himself off the floor. "*Bo'na, at kveda,*" he said. "So serious. I just want to talk to you some more."

"Why?"

"Because you're pretty."

Maayan crossed her arms and glared, and his taunting grin eventually withered. He lowered his eyes.

"I wish I'd had someone like you to talk to back then."

Whatever hesitations she had — and she had many — his raw vulnerability in that moment overcame her better judgement.

"I should be done by two or three," she said.

He rummaged through his pockets, finally locating a pencil stub. He dumped the rest of the cigarettes out of the box and scrawled something on it, then handed it to her.

"Call me," he said. "There's a kosher café a few blocks over."

Maayan took the cigarette box, fumbling with it for a moment, and then looked up with a mischievous smile.

"But does it have a nice bomb shelter?"

"If not, I can bring some flowers to decorate it."

"Such a gentleman."

"I'm the rabbi's son."

They fell silent again. Maayan looked at the doorway, but didn't step toward it.

"Nu?" Yossi urged. "You left your car in the middle of the road. It's probably got thousands of shekels in tickets on it by now."

Maayan cleared her throat and swept past him through the metal door and up the steps.

"Maayan."

She turned back to see his face peering up at her from around the curve in the staircase.

"What channel?" he asked.

She smiled again.

"One. The live broadcast starts after the twelve o'clock news."

"I'll be watching. Don't get hit by a rocket."

"I'll do my best."

THE SWEETEST THINGS

Mama says that the sweetest things grow in the saltiest places.

She told me this when she gave me the first ripe cherry tomato from the patch of earth in our courtyard. We shared the courtyard with several other families, and my mother spent many hours knitting there, keeping an eye on our plants so they wouldn't get trampled by the children running around. Nonetheless, her cherry tomato plants were destroyed time and again, sometimes by children or stray dogs, and sometimes because we couldn't spare the water. I had never seen my mother as happy as she was when she spotted that first little tomato ripening.

"Amal! Amal! Come quick!" she called, and I rushed outside, forgetting to discard the rag doll I'd been playing with instead of folding laundry as she'd asked me to do. Her face, framed in her cream-colored hijab, was alight.

"Close your eyes and open your mouth," she instructed me. I eyed her in suspicion. My brothers had played this trick on me in the past and I'd ended up spitting out a live cricket.

"Just do it!" she insisted, and I obeyed — but not without peeking through one squinting eye. I glimpsed a flash of ruby red as she dropped the tomato into my mouth.

"Chew," she said, and I will never forget the sensation of that fruit bursting with tart sweetness when my teeth broke the skin.

"It's like candy!" I choked a little on the acidic juice.

"The salty earth makes them very sweet," she said.

"Where does the salt in the soil come from?" I asked her.

She sighed deeply. "From all our tears," was her reply.

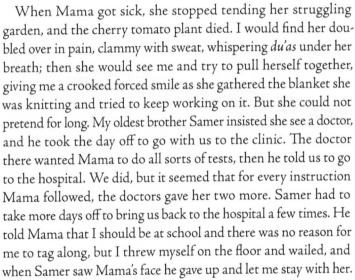

When Mama got sick, she stopped tending her struggling garden, and the cherry tomato plant died. I would find her doubled over in pain, clammy with sweat, whispering *du'as* under her breath; then she would see me and try to pull herself together, giving me a crooked forced smile as she gathered the blanket she was knitting and tried to keep working on it. But she could not pretend for long. My oldest brother Samer insisted she see a doctor, and he took the day off to go with us to the clinic. The doctor there wanted Mama to do all sorts of tests, then he told us to go to the hospital. We did, but it seemed that for every instruction Mama followed, the doctors gave her two more. Samer had to take more days off to bring us back to the hospital a few times. He told Mama that I should be at school and there was no reason for me to tag along, but I threw myself on the floor and wailed, and when Samer saw Mama's face he gave up and let me stay with her.

So I was there when the doctor came in and pulled up a stool by Mama's bed, running his free hand through his cropped black hair. He sat there for a moment, not saying a word, and I saw Samer's knuckles, clutching the rail of the hospital bed, turn white.

"*Hada gadha' allah w gadroh*," the doctor said, and Samer's knuckles turned even whiter. "Allah has ordained it. Your mother," the doctor continued, "has a tumor in her small intestine. The good news is that it might be operable; the bad news is that you need a specialist, and the doctors here in Gaza aren't good enough. She will have to go to Israel."

I burst into tears.

"No, no, *ya amoorti*, don't cry," the doctor said, turning kind eyes on me and reaching out to stroke my cheek.

"But Israel is the enemy! You want to send my mother to the enemy? The Jews will kill her!"

"Amal —" My brother's voice was strained.

"This is something that is done quite often," the doctor went on, turning to Samer. "It's safe. Patients get very good care there. You would be in capable hands. We'll need to request permission, and the process is not always smooth, but under these circumstances…" His eyes flicked back toward me. "I'm fairly confident they will give it quickly. There are organizations on their side that help with the transportation and other arrangements."

There was a long pause, and then Samer finally cleared his throat. "But we can't afford —"

"The Israeli government pays for it."

My mother and Samer exchanged glances, their brows deeply furrowed.

"Why would the Israelis kill my husband without blinking an eye," my mother finally said, "but pay to save my life?"

The doctor stood from his stool, tucking my mother's chart under his arm. "Does anything else in our lives make sense?"

The surgery would either save my mother's life or end it — and nobody knew which was more likely. The adults wouldn't tell me this, but I knew. I could tell because before Mama left she held me in her arms for the longest time, clutching my head to her chest where I could hear her heart beating, and she made the soil saltier for the tomatoes, and before she got up to get in the taxi with Aunt Jamila she whispered: "Promise me that you will always use your strength to make things grow, and never to destroy them." She would not leave until I promised.

In the days that followed, I went to school in the mornings but I spent most of my time there staring out the window thinking about Mama. In the afternoons I would come home to an empty house. Samer didn't like me spending so much time alone, so he told my cousins down the street to keep an eye on me. They coaxed me out to play in the outskirts of the village, on top of a dune overlooking the Jewish settlement that blocked our access to the seashore. I wasn't interested in my cousins' activities; they were a few years older, young teenagers, and they were all boys — so they liked to spend their afternoons chain-smoking cigarettes and *nargila* and catcalling girls. So I ignored them and collected sticks to jab into the sand and pretend I was planting a garden, and when I got bored of that, I would sit on the dune looking at the greenhouses beyond the barbed wire.

Mama had told me about greenhouses. They were like magic houses of eternal summer, she said, using the sunlight to warm the plants and make things grow better than they would in the cold. "Can you imagine?" she would say, her eyes bright as she shook out a bedsheet and hung it on the laundry line in the courtyard. "Strawberries in winter! My grandfather wouldn't have believed it if he'd seen it with his own eyes. Why, the first time your father came back from the greenhouse with strawberries —" She would fall silent then, swallowing, and turn her eyes away so I wouldn't see them welling with tears.

Mama told me never to go anywhere near the Jewish settlement. She told me that was how my father was killed — shot because he got too close to the Jews and their greenhouses. But one day when I was done playing on the sand dune I noticed something strange: the buildings I remembered seeing behind the greenhouses seemed to have disappeared. I begged my cousin Taysir to lend me his old binoculars to get a better look, but they didn't help. So I snuck right up to the barbed wire, and I was amazed by what I saw. The settlement was completely empty, every building except the greenhouses was gone, nothing but piles of rubble on the ground! Had the Jews finally left? Maybe God had finally heard our prayers and Palestine was free! I ran back to my cousins to tell them the good news, but they sneered and told me I was being stupid, that it was only the Jews living in the Gaza Strip who were leaving. I couldn't understand why that wasn't something to be happy about, but they just laughed at my excitement, so I walked away pouting and nursing my pride.

Still, if the Jews had left their houses, that meant that the greenhouses were empty too — and they were still there. Maybe we could use them! I fantasized about taking my mother there after her surgery, walking her blindfolded into the greenhouses, uncovering her eyes, and seeing her laugh and clap her hands the way she did when she was too delighted for words.

Mama's surgery was planned for September 10th. I remember the date because Uncle Ahmed marked it in red on the calendar on his refrigerator, and I studied it many times a day, trying to calculate how long it would be until Mama would get home. They told me it might take several weeks for her to recover enough to come back home. I didn't say so, but I couldn't believe it would take that long. Mama was strong. She would get right up and come back to me. If she survived, I figured she would be back home in three days at most.

Aunt Jamila called on September 10th to tell us that Mama had made it through the surgery. I asked to speak to Mama and Aunt Jamila said she was still sleeping. But I read in Uncle

Ahmed's frown what he would not tell me: something was wrong. I heard him whisper something about bleeding and infection when Samer came to walk me home that evening. I tried asking Samer, but he scolded me for asking too many questions.

Three days later, I was playing on the dune after school when I noticed a crowd of people around the greenhouse on the other side of the fence. At first my heart sank, thinking the Jews were back; but then I saw the big hole in the barbed wire. Several men were carrying heavy boxy things through the hole up toward our village.

I ran over to them and asked what they were doing. They ignored me and continued dragging the objects — which I now know were probably ventilators — up the hill. I stared into the hole they had cut in the barbed wire, my eyes wide. There it was, the forbidden world, open to me at last! After a moment's hesitation, I stepped inside.

The greenhouses were full of men, all very busy. At first I was delighted — maybe they were planting things! But as I drew closer I began to understand what was happening, and my heart sank. Men from my village were carrying off the plastic sheeting and taking apart the irrigation hoses. There were a few Palestinian Authority policemen scattered around trying in vain to stop them, but they were so outnumbered, most of them had given up and were sitting on the ground outside the greenhouses with their heads in their hands as the looters hauled off the equipment.

"Stop it," I heard myself say. "Stop it!" I ran toward one of the men who was rummaging through a pile of hoses and grabbed his arm. "You're ruining the greenhouses!"

The man just shrugged me off.

"Stop it!" I shrieked, stamping my foot as tears splashed down my cheeks. I had promised my Mama that I would use my strength to make things grow, and here they were, ruining this magic building of eternal summer where Mama could have grown cherry tomatoes to her heart's delight.

Overcome with rage, I charged forward and bit the man on his arm.

He bellowed in surprise and pain and flung me to the ground. "What are you, an animal?!" He followed up with a string of curses and threats.

I scrambled up from the sand and ran away crying, the fresh scrapes on my elbows throbbing.

When I had calmed somewhat, I looked up at my surroundings. The rest of what had been the Jews' settlement was now just piles of broken stuff. I picked my way through the debris, heading toward the inviting seashore that had been forbidden to me for so long — but a sudden flash of green made me stop short. I squatted down to examine it. Here, by one of the destroyed houses, was a seedling. I didn't know what type of plant it was; a few long, narrow leaves poked up toward the sky. It had clearly been planted only a short time ago, judging by fairly fresh dirt piled up around it. It looked a little tired, leaf tips brown at the edges, probably because it hadn't been watered properly in a while, but it was still very much alive.

I glanced over my shoulder at the greenhouse, and then back down at the plant.

Using my hands and fingernails, I dug up the seedling, careful to keep the roots intact like Mama had showed me. When I managed to gently pull it out of the ground, I hugged the mess of roots to my chest — getting dirt all over my pink dress — and made my way back to the hole in the fence, joining the last few looters returning to our village. I did not walk back to Uncle Ahmed's. I walked home instead, straight to our courtyard where the tomato plants had died and my Mama had salted the soil with her tears to make the sweetest things grow.

I dug a hole big enough for the seedling, placed the bundle of roots inside, and covered it with dirt. Then I ran to fetch some water in a cup and poured it gently around the base of the plant.

There I sat, my hands caked with mud, salting the soil some more as I waited for Mama to come home.

בַּמַּרְאָה

מַעְיָן צוּרִים

בַּמַּרְאָה אֲנִי רוֹאָה
אָחוֹת תְּאוֹמָה
שֶׁמֵעוֹלָם לֹא הָיְתָה לִי.
אִם אֲנִי מְחַיֶּכֶת, הַאִם גַּם הִיא מְאֻשֶּׁרֶת?
אִם אֲנִי בּוֹכָה, הַאִם גַּם הִיא כּוֹאֶבֶת?
וְאִם הַחַלּוֹן הַזֶּה שֶׁמַּפְרִיד בֵּינֵנוּ
יִתְנַפֵּץ לָנוּ בַּפָּנִים
הַאִם גַּם הִיא?
וְגַם אֲנִי?

In the Mirror

Maayan Tzurim

In the mirror I see
The twin sister I never had.
If I smile, is she happy too?
If I cry, does she hurt too?
And if the window that separates us
Shatters in our faces
Will she shatter too?
And will I?

AUTHOR'S NOTE

I n August of 2005, the State of Israel withdrew its forces and around 8,000 residents from the Gaza Strip and five small settlements in northern Samaria. Neve Adva is a fictional settlement, but its story is based on that event, which was called "the disengagement".

Jewish settlement in Gaza began with Jonathan the Hasmonean, who conquered the area in 145 BCE. Archeological evidence confirms that there was a large Jewish community in Gaza City during the Mishnaic and Talmudic periods (circa 200 – 500 CE). Ruins of an ancient Mishnaic-period synagogue with a magnificent mosaic floor were found near the port; and one of the pillars of the Great Mosque was carved with the Jewish symbols of the menorah, the shofar, and the etrog (citron), with the name "Hanania Bar-Yaacov" in Greek and Hebrew underneath. This engraving was discovered in 1870, and was defaced by Arab nationalists in 1987 at the time of the outbreak of the First Intifada.

The Jewish community in Gaza waxed and waned throughout the Middle Ages. The sage and poet Rabbi Israel Najara was chief rabbi of Gaza and was buried there in 1625. The notorious false messiah Shabtai Zvi was "crowned" in the synagogue of Gaza in 1660. Napoleon's failed attempt to conquer the Holy Land devastated the city, forcing the Jews to abandon it at the turn of the 19th century. Over the next 200 years, Jews returned to Gaza and were forced to leave it several times due to wars and pogroms.

After Israel captured the Gaza Strip from the Egyptians during the 1967 Six Day War, the Israeli government made a concerted effort to reestablish a strategic Jewish presence in the region that would disrupt the continuity of Palestinian settlement. To do this, they established five main areas of Jewish settlement scattered throughout the strip — known as the "Five-Finger Plan". One of those areas was the Gush Katif settlement bloc in the southern region of the Strip. One of the masterminds behind this plan was General Ariel Sharon.

Like many Israeli generals, Ariel Sharon went into politics after retiring from the army. In 2001, during the dark days of the Second Intifada and its frequent suicide bombings, he was elected prime minister on a platform promising a tough approach to security and peace negotiations. He visited the Gaza Strip on May 5th, 2001, in solidarity with the settlers there — who were living with near-daily attacks in the form of mortars and missiles, rocks and Molotov cocktails hurled at their cars on the roads, and drive-by shootings. When he was reelected in 2003, he explicitly stated, "The fate of Netzarim [a Jewish settlement in Gaza] shall be the same as the fate of Tel Aviv."

However, in the months that followed, he had a change of heart. At the Herzliya Conference on December 16th, 2003, he announced that should the latest round of peace talks fail, he would implement a plan for unilateral withdrawal from some of the settlements over the Green Line. His hope was that it would reduce friction in the region, create a stronger defensive front to fend off terror attacks, and strengthen Israel's position in the international community.

The proposal caused a tremendous uproar on the political right. A significant portion of the population — including the majority of Sharon's own political party — was strongly opposed to unilateral withdrawal. Sharon engaged in some dubious political maneuvering to get the plan approved in the Knesset. There were many demonstrations, some of them violent, and vicious rhetoric was launched in both directions. A deep and painful fracture emerged within Israeli society between proponents and opponents of the plan.

Despite the opposition, the plan eventually passed. It was implemented over the course of five days: August 15th – 20th, 2005. It began on the day after Tisha B'Av, the traditional Jewish day of mourning the destruction of the Holy Temple in Jerusalem and other national calamities.

Because of the haste with which the proposal was passed, the resettlement of evacuees was planned and executed poorly. Many residents were stranded in terrible conditions for many months or even years before finally being resettled. Nine years later, in 2014, 40% of the evacuees were still living in "temporary housing", and as of August 2016, 180 families had still not moved into permanent homes.

While the evacuation itself went relatively smoothly and with little violent resistance, the images on television were harrowing, and the event was burned into the hearts of many Israelis as deeply traumatic.

In terms of Sharon's security goals, history — so far — has shown a mixed result: Israeli deaths resulting from conflict in the Gaza Strip fell by about 50%, but frequent wars with Hamas, the radical terrorist group that took over the Strip in 2007, have resulted in severe disruptions and the endangerment of millions of Israelis in Israel proper. The international community briefly applauded the disengagement from Gaza, but the goodwill it created was short-lived, and Israel continues to be blamed for the humanitarian crisis in Gaza because of its tough border control and harsh military responses to missile fire, infiltration attempts, and arson attacks from within the Strip.

The larger societal implications of the event are even harder to assess.

———— ∿∿ ————

I had just graduated high school when the disengagement took place.

The school I had attended was a Bnei Akiva high school, associated with the Zionist-religious community that identified strongly with the settlement movement. While political indoctrination was forbidden, the atmosphere in the school was clearly anti-disengagement, and the pain and the fear felt by those opposing it was palpable.

At home, there was an orange ribbon (in protest against the disengagement) tied to the antenna of my mother's car, while my father's car flew the blue-and-white ribbon (in support of it). Though I was officially opposed, I was ambivalent, never completely agreeing with one side or the other.

I spent those five days shut up in my room in central Israel, refusing to watch the footage of the evacuation or to read about it on the news (a bit like Olga in "Erosion"). The raw pain and confusion and conflicting feelings were too overwhelming for me. My dad — the one who supported the disengagement — was glued to the TV throughout those five days, and what he saw on the screen affected him deeply. He told me at the time about a dream he had that involved meeting an old friend from Pittsburgh — the home we had left nine years before — and an overwhelming sense of sadness, the feeling that he could never go home again. (When I told him I was writing a story based on the concept of this dream, he couldn't recall having it.)

A couple years after the disengagement, I wrote a short story about a female soldier evacuating a widow from a fictional settlement in Gaza. I based it on things I had heard about what had happened, snippets here and there, and on my general impression of the events. In 2016, I decided to rewrite the story, but I knew I would need to do proper research this time. That meant finally exposing myself to the materials I had refused to see eleven years before.

The more I watched, the more I read, more and more conflicting voices rose within me, building up to an awful cacophony. There were so many perspectives, so many raw emotions, so many things to be said, sometimes completely at odds with one another. I felt crippled by the need to select just one angle for my story, and despaired that readers would not be able to fully appreciate what the disengagement meant for Israel by seeing only one perspective.

Then I realized that I didn't have to choose: I could write a story for each one of those voices.

That is how this book was born.

Disengagement is an exploration of the deep ruptures the disengagement tore in Israeli society; but more than that, it's an expression of the ruptures the disengagement tore within me.

GLOSSARY

Aliyah (Hebrew): Literally "rising up"; used also to mean immigration to Israel, or being called up to the Torah reading during prayer services.

Amoorti (Arabic): My dear one.

Baruch Hashem (Hebrew): Thank God.

Boker tov (Hebrew): Good morning.

Datlash (Hebrew): Acronym for dati l'she'avar, meaning "formerly religious," often used as a noun describing a person who left the religious fold.

Gomel blessing: A Jewish blessing recited when one has survived a life-threatening situation, in thanks for being spared.

Hashem Yikom Damo (HY"D): May God avenge his blood. This expression is used to refer to those who were killed specifically because they were Jewish.

Havdalah (Hebrew): The Jewish ceremony performed at the closing of the Sabbath after nightfall on Saturday.

Hesder (Hebrew): A program for young religious men in Israel that combines mandatory army service with religious study.

Khali (Arabic): My cousin.

Ma nishma? (Hebrew): "What's up?" (Literally, "What's heard?")

Nefesh B'Nefesh (Hebrew; literally, "soul in soul"): An organization founded in 2002 that assists Jews in immigrating to Israel ("making aliyah"—see aliyah).

Neshama (Hebrew): Literally "soul", used as a term of endearment.

Piguah (Hebrew): Terror attack

Sabah an-noor (Arabic): "A morning of light." Typical response to "good morning" (sabah al-kheir).

Shalom (Hebrew): Literally "peace"; used as a greeting.

Shalom aleichem/Aleichem shalom (Hebrew): The more formal version of the greeting: "Peace be upon you", with the traditional reply: "Upon you, peace".

Shukran (Arabic): Thank you

Ulpana (Hebrew): Religious high school for girls.

Yishuv (Hebrew): General word for a city or town, often used to mean "settlement".

Yeshiva (Hebrew): A religious school. See also hesder.

Yimach Shema/o (Hebrew): May her/his name be erased. Used to upon pronouncing or hearing the name of a historical enemy of Israel.

ABOUT THE AUTHOR

Daniella Levy was born in New York, but the first home she remembers was in the Jewish community of Squirrel Hill, Pittsburgh. Her family immigrated from there to Israel when she was a child.

Her debut novel, *By Light of Hidden Candles*, was published by Kasva Press in 2017. She is also the author of *Letters to Josep: An Introduction to Jewish Life*. Her short stories, articles, and poetry — in English, Hebrew, and Spanish — have been widely published in literary magazines, anthologies, and other platforms, and she's been nominated for the Pushcart Prize for her short fiction. (Don't ask her about the Spanish. She's not sure how that happened either.)

Daniella blogs about life as a religious Jew living in Israel at LetterstoJosep.com, and about resilience in the face of rejection for artists and writers at RejectionSurvivalGuide.com. She currently lives in Tekoa, Israel, with her husband and three sons.

Follow Daniella:

Website: daniella-levy.com
Facebook: facebook.com/daniellalevyauthor
Instagram: instagram.com/daniellalevy.author
Twitter: @DaniellaNLevy

Acknowledgements

First and foremost, as always, I thank the First and Foremost: the Ultimate Author of history, whose presence and perceived absence bring both comfort and deep pain to the characters in this book and to all the pieces of me that inspired them.

Secondly, I thank my husband Eitan, who — not unlike Rabbi Shlomo — swept me off my feet to a little caravan beyond the Green Line and immersed me in this paradoxical reality we live as "settlers". Most of the marriages in this book are harmonious, loving, and supportive, and, well, they say to write what you know...

Next is my "patron saint" Abigail Levitt, who not only continues to force/inspire me to keep writing and follow my dreams, but also helped develop my understanding of and empathy for one of the viewpoints that had been previously inaccessible to me. On that note, I wish to thank the individuals she put me in touch with who have since become my friends — the one and only Julian Maswadeh (yaaaaas queen!) and dear Ahmed Fouad Alkhatib — for their insights and contributions to "The Sweetest Things". Abi also brought me extremely valuable feedback on that chapter from Nasr Jumaa and Malak Mattar. *Shukran ktir,* and may only sweet things grow between our peoples.

I am eternally grateful to my parents, Jill and Jeff Shames, for bringing me to the land of Israel as a child, and giving me the gift of growing up here. This book would never have existed, on multiple levels, if they hadn't made that difficult and courageous step. I would also like to thank my in-laws, Mark and Nisa Levy, my sister Yonit Arthur, and the rest of our family, for their faithful and constant support.

My deepest thanks to the good folks at Kasva Press, Don Radlauer and Yael Shahar, for seeing what this book could be and helping me get it there. Thanks as well to my "writing chevrutot" Gahl Pratt Pardes and Adina Kopinsky, and to Anne Gordon. Their sharp and insightful feedback has made my writing better.

Ari Moshkovski volunteered as my envoy to the rare books room of the Har Etzion Library when I asked for details on a certain edition of Abravanel's commentary on the early prophets. Ari's extremely detailed play-by-play of this encounter allowed me to accurately describe the 330-year-old tome in the chapter named after it, which (in my humble opinion) added a wonderful air of mystery and historical significance to the scene. Thanks, Ari!

And last but certainly not least: my children, Hallel, Raviv, and Ro'iel, helped me see the world through the eyes of the children in this book. I pray that they will grow up in a world where the happiest ending I could imagine for this story will be their reality.

QUESTIONS FOR DISCUSSION & REFLECTION

1. Why do you think the Israeli government chose to call this operation a "disengagement" as opposed to "withdrawal", "pullout", or "evacuation"? What are some of the other "disengagements" that take place throughout the book?

2. One of the important themes of *Disengagement* is encountering and learning from the Other. Who is the "Other" in the book?

3. Many of the characters in *Disengagement* leave their homes during the story — some more literally than others. Do you think Ehud "leaves home" in some sense during the story? What about Tali, the female soldier? And Hedva, the cantankerous neighbor?

4. In what ways is Reuben's immigration to Israel "leaving home", and in what ways is it "coming home"? His story is structured in two "acts", each with a very different tone; why do you think the author chose to tell his story like that?

5. There are several sets of siblings in the book: Olga and Svetka, Itzik and Joel, Benny and his sisters. How do you

think their relationships reflect the political conflict around the disengagement?

6. Dreams appear as a recurring theme throughout *Disengagement*. In her letter to God, Talia writes: "We're still here in the Land of Israel, living the dream, but burying the dream…" What dreams are the characters living, and what dreams are they burying?

7. The chapter titled "Sacrifices" opens with a visit from Prime Minister Ariel Sharon, and closes with a public announcement he makes. How does this "frame" around the story of Aharon's death help us understand how Shlomo and Shulamit feel about Sharon's change of heart?

8. The anti-disengagement movement referred to the event as an "expulsion", partly to echo tragedies from Jewish history that they felt were parallel to it. In the book, comparisons are made to the expulsion of the Jews from Spain in 1492 and the Holocaust. Do you think these comparisons are fair? Do you think the anti-disengagement movement helped or harmed their cause by making these comparisons?

9. Why do you think Talia felt an obligation to be "an embodiment of the strength of the Jewish people…a symbol of everything we stand for"? Do you think this perceived responsibility helped her, harmed her, or maybe both?

10. Many of the characters in *Disengagement* are or were religious at some point, and many of them struggle with faith as a result of the suffering they've endured. What different reactions to this struggle do we see among the cast of characters?

11. Why do you think Peduel is so ambivalent about Ayala when he first meets her? And why do you think he ends up turning to her for comfort after his experience in Neve Adva?

12. When Yossi tells Maayan that he gets the sense she is criticizing the secular worldview, she replies that she gets the sense that he is asking her to. Why do you think she said that? Why might Yossi be asking Maayan to criticize his worldview?

13. Do you think Amal's mother will come home in the end? How does the note of cautious, open-ended hope of the ending reflect the greater political context of the story?